MANDEIGHT AND THE APPRENTICE MAGE

Book One of the Mandeight Chronicles

Stu Venable

angryfolkstudio.com

Copyright © 2020 Stu Venable

All rights reserved

The characters and events portrayed in this book are fictitious. Any similarity to real persons, living or dead, is coincidental and not intended by the author.

No part of this book may be reproduced, or stored in a retrieval system, or transmitted in any form or by any means, electronic, mechanical, photocopying, recording, or otherwise, without express written permission of the publisher.

To Allegra and Zachary.

CONTENTS

Title Page
Copyright
Dedication
Mandeight and the Apprentice Mage   1
Prologue   2
Chapter One   5
Chapter Two   12
Chapter Three   18
Chapter Four   24
Chapter Five   30
Chapter Six   39
Chapter Seven   45
Chapter Eight   56
Chapter Nine   59
Chapter Ten   74
Chapter Eleven   86
Chapter Twelve   93
Chapter Thirteen   107
Chapter Fourteen   118
Chapter Fifteen   129
Chapter Sixteen   147

Chapter Seventeen	157
Chapter Eighteen	165
Chapter Nineteen	174
Chapter Twenty	184
Chapter Twenty-One	190
Chapter Twenty-Two	196
Chapter Twenty-Three	202
Chapter Twenty-Four	207
Chapter Twenty-Five	216
Chapter Twenty-Six	222
Epilogue	227
Afterword	231
About The Author	233
Books In This Series	235

MANDEIGHT AND THE APPRENTICE MAGE

Book One of the Mandeight Chronicles

by Stu Venable

PROLOGUE

Basma, Cardinal Mage of the South, from the Sovereign Duchy of Eldemy, stood before the ancient, ornate mirror.

"What is it, Cardinal Mage?" his young apprentice asked. She was tall, but not nearly as tall as Basma, who was considered a mountain of a man. As she was training to become a war mage, her dark brown hair was cropped short.

Basma, a tall, portly man with long gray hair was examining the contents of a small wooden chest. He gazed at the glass orbs within, their ancient enchantments reflecting in his brown eyes. He wore robes of white and gold, with a red sash denoting his rank and title.

"I have no idea what it was called when it was first created, Talina, but I call it a skipping mirror," Basma said in a gravelly voice, the result of a long and hard life, and more than one battlefield injury. A scar stretched from the center of his throat to his left ear.

"The enchantments are intricate," she said, approaching the mirror. "When was it created?" she asked.

"I'm not certain, but it is definitely work from the hands of a craftsman of the Second or Third Age of the Old Empire. We know that much by the engravings along the frame. This section here," he said, putting on his spectacles and running a finger along the side of the ornate frame, "is written in the ancient language of magic. It's not been used since the fall of the Old Empire."

"How will this get us to the dark mage?" she asked.

"Better to show than tell, Talina," he said, smiling. "I've arranged for you to accompany me once we return to Eldemy," he announced, expecting excitement from his apprentice.

But she wasn't excited. She felt fear. "Are you sure I'm ready?" she asked.

Basma turned to look at his apprentice. She was young and beautiful. She wore the black robes of an apprentice mage. Her features were sharp, and her dark eyes, normally wise beyond her years, were filled with dread.

"You graduated from the Collegium three years ago, and you've served me as apprentice for nearly eight years. I believe you're ready," he said, reassuringly.

"Besides, I've already told His Grace that he should consider you for the position of Cardinal Mage of the South when I retire, or fall," he said ominously.

Talina looked at her mentor with concerned eyes.

"Don't talk like that, Cardinal Mage. You have many years of service to give to His Grace," she said.

Basma smiled warmly. Most who knew Basma's reputation would be surprised with such warmness, for he was the foremost battle mage in the Sovereign Duchy. His magical might had laid low the mendicant armies from the Sea of Sand. His fiery magic had dispersed five thousand northmen, turning an uprising into a minor riot.

Talina knew the real Basma, not the legendary war mage. He was her teacher. He was her mentor. He was her surrogate father.

"All lives end, Talina, even mine. I have trained you to the best of my ability. You have a talent with the Force of fire that rivals mine. I am confident that you can replace me. In fact, I believe that you may surpass me," Basma said.

"I don't want to think about you dying, Cardinal Mage," Talina admitted.

"Even the most powerful mage cannot defeat death, Talina," Basma said.

Talina looked at her mentor. He had become her father. Her true father had forsaken her when she showed magical talent. She was abandoned to the Collegium to learn the magical art, and she was assigned to Basma as his apprentice.

Now her mentor, the Cardinal Mage of the South, the most powerful war mage in memory, was growing old. He was still a powerful mage, but he was becoming frail. He didn't realize it, nor did most who knew him, but Talina saw it. She noted his failing memory. She noted that he would have to cast spells more than once to make them work.

Talina knew his days were numbered, and at the worst possible time. There was a dark mage. A powerful necromancer had risen to prominence. Most people didn't realize it, but for those who understood the signs, a new dark age was approaching.

She didn't want to admit that she could sense Basma's mortality, but she also didn't want to disappoint him.

"I will serve His Grace as best I can when the time comes, Cardinal Mage. I will strive to make you proud," Talina said.

CHAPTER ONE

I had decided to climb to the highest peak on Ecota Isle to enjoy an aerial view of the harbor. The sunlight danced on the choppy waves within the harbor, causing the water to glitter from this distance. I turned to each cardinal direction and saw nothing but deep blue ocean.

From this height I couldn't make out the walkways the crisscrossed the city surrounding the harbor. In between the structures were buildings of every sort and size, and surrounding all of it was the dull white sand that covered most of the island.

It was a cloudless spring day, not that the seasons mattered here. It was nearly always warm and breezy, except for the few rainstorms that would quickly pass overhead a few times a year, usually during what the locals laughingly called winter.

This was very nearly paradise, at least as far as the weather was concerned, but this, the farthest of the Far Isles, offered little in the way of creature comforts, and those it did offer were expensive. So not much of a paradise really, at least for someone like me, a mage.

When I was much younger, and a student at the Collegium Magicum, I was destined for a life of influence and creature comforts. That never happened. I was marked as unfit for further magical training.

In fact, the Masters of the Collegium regretted teaching me anything. They tried to capture and imprison me. That's how I ended up here, far from the Collegium, far from Duke Elkis' guards, far from the Sovereign Duchy of Eldemy.

My name is Mandeight. My last name isn't important, and I tend to keep it secret: makes me harder to track down. I still considered myself a mage, as do the people who hire my services, even though the law of Eldemy does not.

I spied the cutpurse as I rounded a bend on my way down the mountain. The path was steep and the switchbacks were numerous. I could see the natural harbor in the distance and the bustling city that surrounded it. It was a beautiful sight and well worth the climb, but there were more pressing matters at hand.

The cutpurse was three switchbacks below me, hiding behind a large boulder.

I picked up my pace and walked more lightly, so as not to betray my quickened pace.

As luck would have it, the cutpurse did not peek around the rock as I approached. I crouched low and leaned against the rock, so when the cutpurse peeked again, I would be out of sight.

It didn't take long for the cutpurse to come out from her hiding place, trying to discover where I went. That's when I discovered the cutpurse was a she, by the way.

She wore a tattered shift that must have been white at some point in the distant past. Her skirts were tattered and stained at the bottom, as they were made for a woman much taller. She looked to be in her fourteenth or fifteenth year. There were smudges of dirt on her pretty face, and her hair, which might have been red, was a matted mess.

She was thin, too thin in fact. I would have put her on the verge of starvation.

I watched her as she walked past the rock onto the path.

"You should know better than to try to sneak up on a mage, girl!" I said with a booming voice.

She nearly jumped out of her skin with a high-pitched yelp. She spun to face me, wide-eyed. There was a small dagger in her hand.

I looked at the dagger. She was quick, I'd give her that. She'd reached for it instinctively when I surprised her. Most people wouldn't have the presence of mind to do that.

"I wasn't sneaking, master mage," she said, straightening herself and bowing.

"It's too late for niceties," I said, brandishing my staff. "I should take you to the reeve. He knows how to handle cutpurses."

"I'm not cutpurse!" she said, offended.

"Oh, you're not are you? Then why were you hiding?" I demanded.

"I wanted to see if you would disappear," she explained.

I looked at her with confusion.

"What do you mean?" I demanded.

She pointed further down the path, at the next switchback. The air around the switchback shimmered ever so slightly, a telltale sign of an enchantment. Had I not been so intent on watching this cutpurse, I might have missed it entirely and triggered whatever spell had been bound to that area.

I turned back to her, eyeing her. "You can see that?" I asked.

She nodded.

"Did you set that trap?" I asked, approaching her while preparing a defensive gesture.

"No, master mage. I'm no mage. Not even an apprentice mage. Not any kind at all," she said while taking a step back.

"Then why did you think I would disappear?" I asked.

"I saw it before. Took my mum," she explained, her face turning sad.

"At that spot?" I asked, indicating the switchback.

"No. There are lots of them about. I've spotted lots of them," she said.

"'Lots of them' you say? How many?" I asked.

"Scores. Maybe hundreds."

"And you've seen people disappear in them?"

She nodded. "Only a few times. Once I saw the one that took my mum, I knew what to look for," she explained.

This interested me on many levels. Firstly, this young girl had some magical talent. Most who do not practice the art of magic cannot see the signs of an enchantment. In fact, it's one of the ways the Collegium Magicum used to determine if someone had such talent.

"How long ago did the enchantment take your mother?" I asked.

"I'm not sure," she said sadly. "Maybe five winters. Maybe more."

"That's tough business," I said, softening my tone. "Let's take a look at it and see if we can dispel it."

I walked down to the enchanted switchback. Whoever had crafted it had attempted to hide it even from mages. Had she not pointed it out, I may have mistaken the shimmering from the heat of the path distorting the air. She may have saved my life, or at least saved me from a dangerous, or embarrassing, situation.

I examined the area from the edge of the enchantment. It was circular.

"Can you tell what it does? Do you know where my mum is?" she whispered.

"No. That's difficult to do without walking into it," I explained. "I'm afraid that might be dangerous."

"You think she might be dead?" she asked quietly.

"I can't say, lass. No way to know. But such enchantments are rarely laid with good intent," I said. "It is possible she met her end, though not for certain," I added.

Her mouth became a straight line and her expression darkened while she stared at the shimmering air.

"They've all got a rock like that," she said, pointing to a river rock set in the center of the circle.

I peered at the rock. The surface of the rock had its own faint shimmer.

"That's likely the focus of enchantment," I said.

She furrowed her brow and looked at me.

"Enchantments are lasting spells," I began. "Most spells create an immediate effect, but some mages, especially very skilled mages, can place spells on an object of permanence, binding the Forces to it."

I held up my staff, and she backed away a bit. "Don't be scared. I'm explaining, not threatening," I said. She relaxed a little.

"My staff has a spell placed upon it to allow me to channel the Forces I summon through it. It has other enchantments that help bolster and control those forces. That's one kind of enchantment. It's a lasting enchantment," I said.

I turned back to the enchanted switchback.

"This, however, is another kind of enchantment. The Forces are bound to the stone, along with a logic spell," I explained.

She gave me that "I don't understand" expression again.

I sighed. "A logic spell contains the Forces of the enchantment until certain events or conditions occur. When they do, the logic spell ends, and the Forces are released to do whatever the enchanter intended. Assuming they were competent, of course," I said.

"How do you dispel it?" she asked.

"Well, the easiest way," I explained while pulling a coin from my purse, "is to trigger the logic spell." I tossed the coin into the circle. Nothing happened.

She looked down at the coin with hunger and longing. Clearly she had not seen nor possessed silver in some time, if ever.

"What's your name, girl?" I asked.

"Jass. Don't remember my family name. It changed when I was little," she answered. She was still staring at the coin.

"Well, Jass, it appears that this logic spell won't trigger with inanimate objects. Perhaps it requires a living creature to walk into the circle," I said.

"I'm not walking in there!" she exclaimed.

I laughed. "Nor do I expect you to." I looked about and spied a small lizard sunbathing on a rock.

I stared at the lizard, and I began summoning Forces. I brought forth the Force of the mind. With my right forefinger, I traced the magical symbol to shape that Force into control, cementing in my mind my intention for the spell.

The lizard turned toward me, raised itself by its forelegs and stared at me.

Not breaking eye contact, I said to Jass, "Do you see that lizard on the rock there? Approach it. Do not come between me and the lizard. We must maintain eye contact. Grab it for me."

"It'll run away. They're fast and hard to catch," she said.

"It won't run, I assure you, Jass. Just bring it here," I said.

She did.

"Now toss it in the circle," I said quietly.

She did, and nothing happened. The lizard landed unharmed within the circle, looked around and scurried into the underbrush beyond the circle.

"Well," I said, sitting down on a nearby rock. "This appears to be a people trap."

"How can you dispel it now?" Jass asked.

"I'm going to unravel the spell," I said.

I held out my staff and moved the end of it into the circle until the tip touched the stone. In my mind I visualized the symbol of the Force of magic. In my mind's eye I could see the intricate lines of the logic spell. It was well-crafted. Through these lines I could see the main enchantment on the stone.

It was even more intricate a spell than the logic spell that held it, and it contained Forces I did not recognize. Some of the lines of the spell were pitch black, while others shone like threads of sunlight, each in the form of symbols I did not recognize. I pulled a charcoal stick from my purse along with a small folded parchment and copied them as best I could. They moved and undulated under the lines of the logic enchantment that contained them, keeping the unknown Forces at bay.

I felt a growing sense of unease as I continued staring at the workings of the inner spell. I suspected these were powerful Forces. And I had no clue what this spell did.

"Are you alright?" Jass asked.

"Huh," I said, opening my eyes. My eyes burned as sweat dripped from my brow. I blinked it away. I was taxing my control of the Forces by simply looking at the spell. What kind of spell was this? No doubt dangerous.

I closed my eyes again and concentrated on the logic spell. I imagined the symbol of the Force of magic again and envisioned myself cutting one of the threads of the logic spell. It unraveled with pop and a whoosh of air.

When I opened my eyes, I was sitting on the ground next to the small river stone. The spell had pulled me toward the circle. It must have moved or destroyed the air within the circle, creating a vacuum and pulling me toward it. I scrambled for the stone and picked it up. On the underside were two runes I didn't recognize. They were probably runes representing the two unknown Forces.

"By the gods and the Forces," I muttered. "I think that might have been some sort of transportation spell, and a powerful one." I wasn't certain how I knew that, but somewhere in my mind, at least that portion of the spell resonated.

"Transportation spell?" Jass asked. She walked forward and offered her hand to help me up. I took it. While she was short and thin, she had a strong grip and used her sparse frame to help me stand.

I pocketed the stone.

"Come, Jass, I need to go back to my rooms and study this," I said.

"I'm not going back to your rooms. I'm no doxie," she said fiercely. She was again holding the small blade at the ready, but now she was close enough to strike.

I smiled and showed her my empty palms. "I didn't say you were. I have no intent to hire ... companionship, not now anyway. Besides, you're far too young."

I began walking. I could feel her eyes staring at me as I walked.

"There's a meal in it for you if you assist me," I called.

I heard her hurry up to follow me.

Soon she was walking beside me as we made our way down the treacherous switchbacks. I decided conversation was in order.

"So your mother disappeared four or five winters ago?" I asked.

"I think so. It's hard to remember. I had neither paper nor quill to keep a diary," she answered sadly.

That was interesting. This island urchin had letters enough to keep a diary? Few her age on this island knew their numbers, let alone their letters.

"What of your father? Did he not come looking for you?" I asked.

"I never knew my father, and my mother wouldn't speak of him," she answered.

"You were born here on the island?" I asked.

"No. My mum said we came here when I was little, but I don't remember that," she said.

"Was she running from something, your mother? Perhaps from your father?" I asked.

"I don't know. She never said why we came here," she replied.

CHAPTER TWO

We sat at my small supper table, staring at the stone. The remnants of our meal, roasted boar, pickled turnips and boiled turnip greens, laid on the table. My landlady had kindly brought the meal from her kitchen across the road. Jass ate it all, even the turnip greens. I didn't know many adults who would eat them. They're an acquired taste. She must have been starving.

My supper table was a typical trestle table made of oak. It had been imported from the city of Eldemy on the mainland long before I got here. The top of the table was nearly three inches thick, and a thick layer of shellac preserved the scratches and gouges that marred its surface.

A cook stove sat in one corner, and a smaller table for preparing meals sat next to it. There were four simple stools, made from some indigenous tree, around the table, but I had only had cause to use one until now.

The whole place was constructed of wood beams and paneling. One would never find such construction on the mainland, for inhabitants of such a home would freeze to death in the winter.

There was another advantage to using such light materials. When the occasional monsoon raged through, there was a good chance I would survive my home collapsing on me. That wouldn't be the case with the stone structures that were so common in Eldemy.

As Jass greedily finished her meal, I took the enchanted stone from my purse.

As I stared at the stone, I asked, "How well do you know your letters, Jass?"

"Alright, I think, though I haven't read in a long time," she said.

I looked her in the eye. She returned my gaze with suspicion. She had a hard face, surely the result of a hard life.

"How did you manage to survive out there?" I asked.

"There's plenty of coconuts and fruits if you know where to look.

Sometimes I bring a basket to market and sell them when I find more than I can eat," she replied.

"And how old were you when your mother disappeared?" I asked.

"I think I was ten when she disappeared. I'm not sure how old I am now," she admitted.

"I would guess you're about fifteen," I said. "So you're telling me you survived out there for five years by foraging fruit and selling the excess? That seems unlikely."

Most orphans her age resorted to crime eventually, and I suspected she did as well.

"Well, there's a big shipwreck on the other side of the island. I sometimes go out there and find things I can sell. I found some muskets and pistols once," she said.

"Where is this shipwreck?" I asked.

Her eyes narrowed, and she said, "I'm not saying. I found it. It's mine."

"Very well," I said, raising my hands in a placating gesture.

"Let's see how much you remember of your letters." I pointed toward a door. Apart from the entrance, there were three doors leading off of this room. One led to my bed-chamber, one to my library and the third lead to what would be Jass's bedchamber if she decided to accept my offer.

"Go through that door, that's my library, and find a book called 'A Treatise on the Forces' by Xavier Birdstaff," I said.

"'Birdstaff?' What kind of name is that?" she asked.

"An unfortunate one. Don't come back until you find it," I said.

It took her less than five minutes to return with the small folio I'd stolen from a library in Ecoja Smurt, a vile, cold town in the northern reaches of the Duchy of Eldemy.

"Very good!" I said. "Now, should you wish to engage me as your mentor, this shall be your first text. You shall copy it down so you have your own copy."

"Mentor? Am I to be an apprentice?" she asked.

"Yes, if you choose to accept my offer. You have talent, young Jass. I will teach you and train you. In return, you will remain in my service until such time that we part."

"'Service?'" she asked suspiciously.

"Yes. Cleaning. Perhaps the landlady can have someone teach you to cook. You can take the room through that door as your own," I said, pointing to the door behind her.

"Just cleaning and cooking?" she asked.

I rolled my eyes. "Yes, just cleaning and cooking. Maybe errands. Fetch me things from the market. Carry messages. Nothing untoward."

She looked at me straight in the eye. Then she sat down and stared off in the distance. This was certainly a surprise to her. I could almost see the gears of her mind working: balancing the risks and rewards, trying to divine any ulterior motives I may have had.

I did have one ulterior motive, as do most mages who take on an apprentice: a free servant. Housemaids aren't cheap, and they charge a rather dear fee here on the Ecota Isle.

It is also exceedingly rare to find a child with magical talent that hasn't already been snatched up by the Collegium. Jass was doubly rare, as she had spotted an enchantment that was specifically designed to thwart detection by mages.

This young Jass might well become a very powerful mage. If she worked at it she could surpass me, and possibly most of the mages I knew.

There was another motive as well. I'm considered an outcast within the Collegium. That is where I received much of my training, but I was expelled before I earned by 'Patents of Magic,' which would allow me to work the art on the mainland.

Mages have always been viewed with suspicion, and rightly so. Many take the left-hand path and work for their own personal gain and acquisition of power. Even patented mages sometimes abuse their access to lords and ladies and other powerful members of society. Not all, certainly, but it happens.

It was the Eldemy Council of Lords, many centuries ago, who wrote the laws establishing the Patents of Magic as a way to control mages. Without such patents, a mage cannot work for hire, whether it be for an ordinary citizen or a high-born lord.

When I was expelled I assumed they would tell me in no uncertain terms that I was no longer welcome on the mainland, but that isn't what happened. They tried to capture me, to imprison me. That's why I lived on this gods-forsaken pirate haven of an island. No such law existed here.

The fact was, this might be my only chance to pass on what I had learned. I would never be assigned an apprentice by the Collegium, and Jass was the only other person I'd met here with magical talent.

"Okay. I'll do it," Jass said, interrupting my train of thought.

"Hmm? Oh, very good," I replied.

"So where in this book do we figure out the stone enchantment?" Jass asked.

"What? No!" I said, laughing. "I'm going to figure out the enchantment. You're going to start copying that book. Your room is over there. There's parchment, quills and ink at the desk. Off you go." I began studying the stone.

I looked up to see Jass frowning at me.

"Off you go. Shoo. I'm magicking," I said. She got up and stormed across the room to her chamber, much in the manner one would expect from a teenager.

The stone was an interesting dilemma. The two runes represented two Forces of magic with which I was unfamiliar.

Forces, always capitalized, allow the mage to summon, change and control various aspects of reality.

There are the Elemental Force: earth, air, fire and water. Each allows a mage to control, create or somehow change these elements. My aptitudes tend toward air and water. I've never been very good at earth or fire. They can also be combined. A mage can make boiling water using the water and fire Forces, though it's much easier to put a kettle over a fire, and safer.

For living things, there are Forces of body and mind, allowing a mage to control, change or manipulate the respective thing. There is also a Force for plants, but few mages show an aptitude for it.

There are also Forces called the Meta Forces. These are the Forces of change: lessening, bolstering, quickening and impediment.

I cannot tell you how many Forces there are, only that I am well-versed in six: air, water, mind, body, lessening and bolstering. I am also aware of, though not proficient with, the Forces of fire, earth, quickening and impediment.

Oh, there is one other Force that all mages learn to one level or another: the Force of magic. This is the Force used to manipulate magic itself. It's used to make or unmake enchantments. It's also used to create magical connections between things and create logic spells. It's so necessary for spell casting that every mage it taught to use this Force, regardless of their aptitude.

Now you may ask yourself, what are these Forces? Where do they come from?

The answer to that question depends on who you ask, but I'll give you my answer, which I believe to be an honest one: no one knows.

You'll get all kinds of answers from different mages, but it's all opinion. Unfortunately, many of these mages consider opinion to be fact. As a result, many young mages find themselves hindered by these wrongheaded theories of what magic truly is.

I've always felt that such theories were intentionally used to hamstring young mages, limit their powers to see if they'll become monstrous dark mages. These theories put impressions in the young mages' minds about the nature and limitations of the Forces.

This is why I started Jass with "A Treatise on the Forces." While Xavier Birdstaff was in many ways a hidebound git, he did understand the importance of avoiding any hard-and-fast definitions of the Forces. Writing that book was probably the one right thing he did.

So I was aware of twelve Forces, and these were called the Common Forces. These were the Forces that all apprentice mages have the opportunity to learn, but certain Forces seem to have affinities to different mages (or perhaps, mages have affinities to certain Forces). Therefore, it was rare for a mage to know all twelve Common Forces, though some do.

Early in my time at the Collegium, rumors spread among the students of several other Forces. Some said they were referred to as the God Forces, but they would have no way of knowing that. The thought of our teachers and mentors hiding secret Forces from us was intriguing.

Many of us mused that such Forces might allow us to perform miraculous magical feats, not that what we were already doing wasn't miraculous. Especially for young mages, though, the idea of secret knowledge was fascinating.

The teachers of course denied the existence of such Forces, which made us all the more curious.

I hadn't thought about the God Forces in years. Furthermore, I'd never come across a text (and I'd read many) that even mentioned such a thing.

But now I was staring at a stone that proved to me that at least two unknown Forces existed, and there was someone out there who knew how to use them and use them well.

This was both fascinating and concerning.

CHAPTER THREE

Summoning, harnessing or manipulating Forces requires great concentration. Forces are like wild horses that must be tamed. It takes great mental discipline to control the Forces, and should a mage fail to do so, terrible and destructive things can happen.

This leads some mages to believe that Forces are spirits or demons, manifestations of the things the Forces represent. But when one fails to control them, the resulting calamities seem far too random to have a conscious mind behind them.

Summoning or bringing up Forces isn't difficult for a mage. It's the control that's critical, so the summoning must be done correctly.

Having seen the runes of the two unknown Forces on the stone, I could probably, given enough time, bring them forth, but I would have no idea how to control them or what they did. Learning such control requires training and practice. Bringing up a Force you do not know how to control is extremely dangerous, and doubly so if you don't even know what that Force does.

And that's the situation I was in.

Experimenting with those runes could be deadly. I knew one had something to do with transportation, or perhaps teleportation, but I had no idea what else it could do.

"Mandeight," Jass asked over a dinner of coconut and rabbit stew, "I have a question about the Forces.
"Good!" I said. "Curiosity is to be encouraged. What's your question?"

"Xavier Birdstaff drew symbols that represent each Force, and there are rhymes to help us picture those symbols in our minds," she started.

"That's correct. Though in time, you won't need to use the rhymes to visualize the symbols. It does take a great deal of practice," I said.

"But why don't we just draw them?" she asked.

I was both pleased and concerned that she had asked such a dangerous question.

"Your question leads to very dangerous information – information no mage willingly shares with non-mages," I started.

She sat up, her expression both curious and eager.

"If I tell you about inscribing these symbols, what I tell you must remain between you and I. You cannot share this information," I cautioned.

"I give you my sacred word," she said. This was a strange phrase for a homeless girl to utter unless she was high-born. Jass was proving to be well-spoken and well-lettered. She possessed an education few low-born would ever have access to unless they were marked to attend the Collegium.

"Very well," I said. "The rhymes are tools we use to accurately visualize the symbols of each Force. They are tried and true ways to picture them in your mind, but the symbols themselves have power.

"In fact, you could draw the symbols for each Force of a spell on the ground, for instance, and cast a spell. It's very time-consuming, obviously, and dangerous if you get them wrong, because inscribing the symbols can harness far more power than visualizing them," I explained.

"Then why don't they start with that? It seems much easier to draw them than to visualize them," she said.

"True, but it's also much more dangerous if you get them wrong, for you are creating a physical representation of the Forces. The runes on the stone we found were inscribed there because that enchantment requires an enormous amount of energy for some reason," I said.

"It still seems safer to draw them than to visualize them," she pressed.

"That leads me to the real secret you must keep: anyone can draw the symbols for the Forces and create spells. You need no magical talent to do so," I said, wondering if I really should have trusted her with this information.

"Really?" she whispered.

"Yes. If that information got out, it would cause pure chaos," I warned.

"How so?" she asked.

"One of the things mages learn in the Collegium, and one of the things I will teach you, is the ethical responsibility of being a mage. This is why such magic is not taught. If the wrong person were to find a text with such knowledge, they could wreak havoc on our world."

"And mages are intentionally not taught how to do this. The Collegium doesn't want anyone writing it down, or teaching it to people who don't understand the responsibilities of magic.

"Only a few mages are taught this kind of magic, as it can be quite potent. I'm told a few battle mages are secretly taught this magic by the Masters of the Collegium, but they only give this knowledge to their most trusted students, and only when they've established themselves in positions of authority and responsibility," I said.

"Do you know how to do this?" she asked.

"No, though I could probably work it out if I had to, were the situation dire enough," I said.

"Have you ever seen it used?" she asked.

"No, but I have heard rumors. There is one particular battlemage. He fought with the Duke's armies during the nomad wars. I'm told he cast a spell like this during a very large battle. He used the Force of earth to increase the gravity on a section of the battlefield held by the enemy. They were crushed to the ground. Many died. A lucky few broke both legs. Some were paralyzed from back injuries.

"They say he incapacitated nearly a thousand footmen and horsemen with that one spell," I said.

"That awful," she said.

"It is," I answered. I was gladdened that the story scared her. I had not seen much kindness yet in young Jass, at least until now. The fact that such a display of magic gave her pause was quite a relief. The last thing a mentor wants to do is teach magic to someone without kindness and empathy. That's how you create monsters.

The next evening, Jass was in her room, still copying the text.

The whole building shuddered, and I felt a blast of heat from Jass's room.

I ran quickly to the door and flung it open. Her chamber consisted of a small bed with a pile of blankets for a mattress. There was a table and chair, and a wardrobe in one corner. Like the rest of my rooms, there were no windows, but there was an oil lamp on the table for reading, as well as two mounted to the opposite wall for general lighting.

But the room was not in the same order as when I had last looked in. The table was smoldering, though there were no actual flames, thankfully, and the chair, along with Jass, was laying next to the wall opposite of the table.

She sat on the floor next to her chair and looked at me sheepishly, and a little stunned. Her red hair was singed at the ends and one of her eyebrows was partially missing.

"Don't skip ahead!" I admonished. "Fire comes much later, and besides, you're supposed to be copying, not experimenting."

I was actually rather terrified. Jass had brought forth the Force of fire, the most dangerous, destructive and painful magical Force, by reading a book. For most mages, being able to do that without instruction was very nearly impossible. There's so much more to it than reciting the various rhymes for the Forces, and that portion was very rarely written down, and for good reason.

She blinked at me.

"Come here," I said, holding the door open for her.

"Sorry," she said as she sat down at the large oak table in my main room.

"I would normally save this talk for later in your training, but clearly, you have considerable talent and enthusiasm, which I laud," I started.

"On the first page of the text, what does the author say? In the very first sentence." I asked.

"Forces of magic are dangerous and hard to control," she recited.

"Exactly. Word-for-word, in fact," I said, muttering the last part to myself. "Clearly you did not believe that when you read it. Do you believe it now?"

"Yes," she said quietly.

"Good. I'd like to tell you a story to drive the point home. Have you ever heard of High Fall?" I asked.

"No," she answered.

"I'm not surprised. High Fall was a city in the southern portions of the Duchy of Eldemy, nestled high in the Wall Mountains. But don't go looking for it. It's not there anymore," I said flatly.

Jass's eyes went wide.

"No, it wasn't my doing. It was a mage – and apprentice mage, mind you – who lived more than one thousand years ago. This is a lesson that's been passed down from mentor to apprentice for thirty generations, perhaps more. And there is some historical record confirming this, so it's not apocryphal.

"This young apprentice grew bored with the thorough learning necessary to master each and every Force. He decided, much like you, to skip ahead. He sneaked into his mentor's library. He was fascinated with earth magic, you see.

"He searched through the library and found his mentor's treatise on the Force of earth. That night, he decided to call up the Force of earth, but he had no idea how to control it. He had already learned to control one or two Forces, and he figured he could use that knowledge and experience to control the Force of earth.

"He lost control of it almost immediately. The Force raged into the mountain upon which the city of High Fall was built, causing a massive earthquake.

"The mountain cracked in half, and the city plunged into the depths of the valleys below. It is believed he killed more than thirty thousand people, including children," I said.

She sat in silence, looking down at her hands, which were folded neatly in her lap.

"Had your experiment gone a little more awry, we might be standing out in the street, watching this place burn," I said.

"I won't do it again," she said quietly.

"Of course you will!" I laughed, "we all do! Hell, I did many times. We all say we won't do it again, but after the memory of the terror of our first mishap fades, we don't mean it," I said with emphasis. A small smile slipped onto my face, and I winked.

She started to crack a smile

"But you don't do it in the middle of a city, especially a crowded city," I said, raising my voice.

"And you don't do it in a wooden building that contains my irreplaceable library. Back when I was studying at the Collegium, they would have taken the switch to me for such a stunt. Hell, what you did wasn't much different than the stunt that got me expelled and banished from my homeland!"

"I understand," she said.

"Good, now get to bed. We're getting up early tomorrow. We have to go to the governor's mansion," I said.

"The governor's mansion? Why?" she asked.

"I need to do some research in the library. I hope you like research because mages do a lot of that," I said.

CHAPTER FOUR

The next morning, after breakfast, which I helped Jass cook, we set off for the mansion of the governor of Ecota Isle. We wended our way along the raised wooden walkways that spared travelers the effort and discomfort of walking on Ecota Isle's white sand.

The mansion was built atop a plateau that loomed over the city surrounding the harbor. It was made of the same white stone used for government buildings in Eldemy, no doubt imported here at great cost centuries before.

Surrounding the mansion was a defensive wall standing nearly twenty feet high, also built from the same white stone. I imagined it took a thousand ships to carry over all those stone blocks. Wide cannon ports broke up the ominous sight of the defensive wall, with the muzzle of each massive gun extending outward toward the harbor and the sea beyond.

Cannons used to defend fixed structures were usually much larger than those carried on ships or pulled by horses to escort armies into battle. This was mostly due to the fact that once they are in place, they'll never be moved again.

I was told that there were thirty-six 68-pound cannons protruding from the wall, though I never bothered to count them.

The whole place had been built to defend the mansion from pirates. It had failed, but I'll get to that in a moment.

Several flights of stairs crossed back and forth up the side of the plateau to the gates in the defensive wall. I didn't relish climbing all those stairs, as I'd just climbed a mountain the day before, and I did that to get myself back in shape. I'm not a very fit man, and I was now at an age where fine food and little exercise took its toll on my waistline and other places.

As I stopped on the wooden walkway that led to the stairs, Jass spoke.

"Would it be alright if I go gather my things?" she asked.

"Your things?" I said.

"Not much, but I have some in a cave over that way," she said, pointing toward a hill on the shoreline, not far from the mansion.

"Certainly," I said. "I'll wait here for you unless you need help."

"I don't," she said quickly. Clearly, she wanted her "home" to remain a secret.

"Very well," I said, "off you go. I'll be here when you get back." My legs were sore from yesterday's hike anyway, and the stairs leading up to the mansion would just make it worse.

She returned less than an hour later, carrying a wide, flat basket that she had obviously woven herself. I glanced at the basket's contents and at once felt very sad and ashamed for looking.

Within the basket were Jass's prized possessions, and it made me realize how truly fortunate I had been in my life.

Within the basket were two large pineapples, a small brass compass (from the shipwreck she had been looting, no doubt), a section of thin rope, some seashells and a ratty doll, no doubt given to her by her parents many years ago.

The doll's head was made of ceramic, but it was cracked and a few pieces were missing. She had pulled strands from the rope to wrap around the doll's head to hold it together. The doll's clothes, which were worn and falling apart, appeared to be a miniature dress, similar to what a highborn lady might wear.

Jass looked up at me, expecting me to say something. I smiled at her. She didn't smile back.

"Once we get to the gates, you can leave your basket with the guard. He is trustworthy, I assure you," I said seriously.

"Are you sure?" she asked.

"Very sure. He used to be a pirate, but he doesn't plunder treasures from young women, only the Duke's ships," I said.

She nodded seriously and we began the long climb to the gates.

I had been told that the gates were always left closed during the last governor's reign, but that was not the case now. The gates stood open wide, the only defense being a retired pirate in an ill-fitting steel corslet, lazily carrying a matchlock musket.

"Hello, Mandeight," the guard said. I'd never gotten his name, but he was a friendly fellow, and knew me well, as I used to come here often.

"Good day to you!" I said. "This is my apprentice, Jass. Could she leave her belongings with you whilst we confer with the minister?"

"Certainly, young miss," the guard said. "My name is Baxton. If I'm not here when you leave, tell whoever is guarding to come fetch me. I'll keep it safe."

His name was Baxton, apparently. He truly was a friendly fellow, as were most of the retired pirates that now defended the mansion and manned its impressive guns.

Truth be told, I had not yet met an unfriendly retired pirate. Working pirates could be right gits, but the retired ones didn't bother acting intimidating. They'd lived a long time in a dangerous profession, and they didn't need to put on airs of intimidation. The fact that they lived to see gray hair in that perilous life was intimidating enough.

We walked across the courtyard to the mansion. It was a two-story structure, all made of that white stone. There was a balcony on the top floor, and from it hung a long-retired pirate flag. It was black, with a white skeletal hand shaped to make a rude gesture. A decade or so earlier, it had been the most feared flag on the seas between here and Eldemy. Now it was the symbol for an upstart governor.

The front doors to the mansion were unguarded and open, just like the gates. We walked in and I approached another retired pirate sitting at a desk, lost in a pile of parchment. I cleared my throat.

"Well, if it isn't Mandeight the Mage! What brings you up here so early?" said the short, rotund man sitting at the desk.

"Greetings, Minister Graybeard. I need to look in the archives," I replied. Minister Graybeard was the right-hand man to Governor Cavil. They were both former pirates. Cavil was a pirate commodore, a captain who commanded more than one ship. He in fact commanded what would be considered a fleet.

About a decade earlier, then Commodore Cavil developed his exit strategy from the dangerous career of piracy. He executed a raid on the governor's mansion and seized control of Ecota Isle and declared himself governor of the newly independent island state. Graybeard had been his loyal quartermaster for many years and eventually was made captain of one of the ships under Cavil's flag (the one with the skeleton hand and the rude gesture).

Graybeard had a great mind for logistics that would rival the most studious ducal bureaucrat, and while Cavil was technically governor, it was Graybeard who kept Ecota Isle a flourishing trade hub and pirate haven.

Once Cavil took the mansion, he put his most experienced gunners on the massive cannons and was able to maintain his hold on power for nearly a decade now. He was even able to repel the fleet the Duke of Eldemy sent to retake the isle. I'd heard that he sunk eight of the duke's galleons and numerous smaller ships. The duke never sent a second fleet.

"What do you need to look in the archives for?" Graybeard asked.

"I believe there may be another mage on this island. He seems to be trapping unwary travelers," I explained.

Graybeards bushy eyebrows knitted into an expression of worry, accentuating the sun-dried wrinkles above his nose.

"Hmm. Well, no one's come to the governor with their patents. Not since we took over, anyways," Graybeard said. "Cavil doesn't bother with such formalities. If he did, he wouldn't have let you ashore."

"True enough," I admitted. "Oh, this is my apprentice, Jass. Jass, may I present Minister Graybeard." Jass performed a reasonable attempt at a curtsy.

"Pleased to meet you, my lord," she said.

"Not a lord, young miss. Only a minister," he corrected with a smile. Pirates, for all their faults, didn't believe in such things as noble birth, and I tended to agree with them on that at least.

"I believe this mage may be quite dangerous," I said. "Whoever it is, they are well-versed in very powerful forms of magic."

"Well, unless they came here before we took over, I'm afraid I can't be much help," Graybeard said.

"I suppose this mage may have come here prior to your revolt, perhaps remaining hidden, masquerading as someone else," I mused.

"We do have the old registries of patents. You're welcome to peruse them. Come with me," he said, struggling to stand.

Graybeard reached for a wooden crutch. He tucked it under his arm and hobbled to the back of the chamber.

Jass stared at the wooden shaft that had replaced is missing left leg. "What happened to him?" she whispered.

"No need to whisper, young miss. I lost it to a twelve-pound cannonball. Took it clean off at the knee, but my hearing is fine," he said, making a cutting gesture with his free hand. "Cavil took a torch to it to cauterize it, to make sure I didn't bleed out. He saved my life that day."

Jass looked wide-eyed and a little sick.

We followed Graybeard down a narrow spiral staircase to the mansion basement, where the official records were kept.

The retired quartermaster set us up at a table with nine aging volumes of the registry of patents. He placed a few lanterns on the table and lit them, giving us some light. Like my rooms in the city, this basement had no windows. Without the lanterns, it would be pitch black here.

I perused the first of the volumes.

"How far back do these go?" I asked.

"Not exactly sure. Haven't had the time to read all of them, but I would guess four or five centuries," Graybeard mused.

"Hmm," I muttered. "This may take us some time," I said apologetically.

"Not to worry. Hardly anyone comes down here but me. Take your time," he said, making his way to the staircase. "Put out the lanterns when you're done."

I produced a small piece of parchment from my satchel. I unfolded it and handed it to Jass.

"This is a long-shot, but these are the runes of the unknown Forces used in that enchantment," I explained. "Many mages include symbols of Forces they have mastered in their signatures. It's a way for mages to convey to each other their talents and specialties.

"While it's unlikely a dark mage would advertise such power, these runes are all but unknown. It wouldn't be that foolish or dangerous to include them. Besides, many mages suffer from hubris, and they can't help but boast," I said.

I handed her four of the nine volumes. "Check each signature carefully. Look for these symbols. They might be hidden among a more intricate design. Make a note of any you think might match.

We set about looking through hundreds of pages of registered patents, and it took us most of the day.

It was near nightfall when I finally finished the last registry.

"I've found nothing," I said with frustration. "How did you fare?"

"Nothing promising," she said, handing me a parchment with two notations.

"What are these?" I asked.

"Two signatures with those symbols, but they're very old," she explained.

"One is from 9702 and the other is from 9530. They're centuries old," she said glumly.

"Those two would be long dead by now," I said, "but let me have a look." I examined her notes.

"Not two. One mage. It's the same signature, or very nearly so," she said.

"That can't be," I said. "That would make them over a hundred and seventy years old."

"Look for yourself. They're the same," she said. She reached for two volumes and immediately turned each to the proper page. Jass, I noted, had a very good memory.

I examined the older entry. The mage's name was Marwoleth, and within the final flourish of his signature were the two runes.

I then checked the other volume. Again, the mage's name was Marwoleth, and the signatures were nearly identical, though separated by more than a century.

The bottom fell out of my stomach. No one lives 170 years. Hell, hardly anyone lives much past 70 or 80 years.

"We need to get back to my rooms. There's an enchantment there to hide us," I said, collecting my things to leave.

"What's wrong," Jass asked as she followed me up the staircase.

"I'm not certain, but if these two signatures belong to the same mage, and this Marwoleth still lives, we could be in grave danger. There's an old rumor that some mages, especially dangerous ones, have learned to extend their lives. It's only a rumor, but I don't want to take any chances. We must hurry," I said.

CHAPTER FIVE

As soon as we arrived at my rooms, I sent Jass to my library to fetch a volume.

I spent the evening casting more enchantments to protect us from scrying, a method by which mages find people and things. My previous enchantments, called scry walls, were good, but I didn't want to take any chances. More enchantments would provide more protection and give me a better chance of a warning that someone was trying to find us.

"Will you please tell me what's going on," Jass said finally. She was at the big oak table in the center of the room, continuing her work copying the Xavier Birdstaff text.

I sat down hard on the stool. I was exhausted from the workings I'd just put down on my rooms.

"There's a secret within the Collegium," I started. "They don't like to talk about it for reasons that will become obvious, and they never speak of it to outsiders."

"That seems to be a trend," Jass said drying.

"It's no joking matter. Not now," I scolded her. "There are some mages who very quickly forget the moral and ethical teachings of the Collegium. These mages use their talents to further their own ends, with no concern for the world around them. They inevitably have their Patents of Magic revoked, not that it means anything to them.

"They are eventually hunted down and are forced to flee the duchy, or they're killed. It's a rare occurrence, but it does happen," I said.

"Did you find that volume I asked for?" I asked.

"Yes," she said. She picked up a small leather-bound book and handed it to me.

Upon the cover of the volume was the title "A List of Mages of Note," inked into the leather and written in my own handwriting many years ago. It was a list of powerful and noteworthy mages, both current and historic. Whenever I came across the record of such a mage, I would make a note of it in this volume, including their name, where they lived, what the historical record claimed they did, any texts they may have written, etc. It was a reference I would take with me any time I had the opportunity to visit a library. Such mages often wrote down their research and musings about magic and having a list of such names helped me find these texts.

The volume had more than a hundred pages within, and all but twenty or so had notations of such mages.

"That name you found, 'Marwoleth.' I may have heard that name before," I said as I paged through the volume.

The earliest entries in my volume were so old the ink was fading, but I found a page with the name Marwoleth written at the top. It was one of my earliest entries.

"Jass. Can you make this out? The light is too dim, and my eyes are too old," I admitted.

She began reading:

"Marwoleth. Collegium graduation date: Unknown. Year 7116: raised an undead army from the ruined city of Amana. Attempted a siege of Eldemy. The siege was broken after two months. Marwoleth evaded capture."

I stared at the flickering flame of the oil lantern on the table. The night was growing cold. I suddenly felt very old, which is surprising since I wasn't yet in my fortieth year.

"Put a couple of logs on the fire, please," I said quietly. Jass got up and did so.

"So who is this Marwoleth?" she finally asked.

"He is one of those mages I spoke about. The ones that choose the selfish path. But this is something different, something worse," I said.

Jass looked at me quietly, waiting for me to continue.

"Marwoleth was a necromancer. A mage who specializes in death magic. Such magics are unknown within the Collegium, but rumors have always persisted that such power was out there for the taking. And there was a historical record of him, so this is more than rumor. There have been no reports, that I have found at least, of a necromancer since Marwoleth's siege of Eldemy, nearly three thousand years ago.

"At the Collegium, there were rumors that necromancers of old could extend their lives. Some said they could transfer their souls into another body. Others said they hid their souls away, keeping them safe, so they could not be killed by traditional means."

"So this Marwoleth," she said, indicating the volume, "might be the same Marwoleth in the registry of patents?"

"Just so, Jass. Just so," I said.

I did not sleep that night. I sat in my bed-chamber monitoring my enchantments, feeling for signs that they had been disturbed or otherwise touched by magic.

I heard Jass busying herself in my rooms early in the morning. She was probably starting a fire in the stove and putting water on to boil. I soon smelled cooking bacon and the scent of slightly burnt toast.

Before I emerged from my chamber, I splashed water on my face and changed into my mage robes. I had not worn them in a long time. My robes were a source of painful memories. I had not finished my studies at the Collegium, and thus, I never received my Patents of Magic.

Technically, I was not allowed to wear the robes of a mage outside of the Collegium.

Mage robes were in many ways a badge of office, an office I did not hold, even though I was more talented than many of those who could wear them.

But I wanted Jass to see the tradition she was joining in its full regalia. It might have seemed silly to an outsider, but the potential presence of this Marwoleth got me thinking.

I was taking on a very serious responsibility, and I hadn't been taking it very seriously. I was teaching this young girl, who was mostly a stranger, a power unrivaled in our world. We had not yet discussed the responsibilities of a mage and the code by which we were supposed to live.

I checked myself in the large looking glass in my chamber. My robes were old and tattered.

Moths had done their worst around the neckline.

I picked up my stole from my days at the Collegium. It consisted of strips of silk dyed white, blue, brown and red, symbolizing the four basic elements: air, water, earth and fire. I affixed the pin of my class, a silver dragon, to my stole where it crossed at my chest.

I emerged from my chamber with a flourish, the lengths of my stole and robes shifting about me.

"We must eat up quickly, Jass. I'm going to show you how to scry," I announced.

Jass was at the stove. She was pulling four eggs from a pot of boiling water with a wooden spoon.

"It's almost ready. There's bread and bacon on the table," she said, not looking up.

I sat down to eat and waited for her to bring the eggs.

As she sat down, I started.

"I have not taught you some important things about magic, and I think I should do so now, especially in light of what we discovered yesterday," I began.

She sat quietly, not eating, and listened.

"The mages of the Collegium do not have a rigid code of conduct, but there are some things you must know. These are things they teach to all of us.

"We ply our craft at the favor of the Duke of Eldemy. Therefore, if we are called to service by the Duke or the nobles beneath him, we give that service without charge. While they may compensate us, we must not demand payment," I said.

I was trying to recite what I had once learned by rote decades before, but I struggled to remember it all.

"Here on this island, we would replace the Duke and his court with the governor and his ministers," I added.

"We do not do violence with our magic unless it is in self-defense or in a time of war," I said, struggling to remember the rest. Had I earned my Patents of Magic, I could simply read them, but I'd never earned them.

"We do not use our magic to settle common grudges. We do no use our magic to supplant the Duke's justice, only to enforce it," I continued.

"While we may employ our art for pay from freeborn citizens, we may not do so to intimidate, cajole, rob, sway the minds of, or otherwise harm freeborn citizens.

"We may not use our art to sway the minds of the Duke or any under his employ," I said. I was now struggling to remember the rest and failing.

"So do I just replace 'Duke' with 'governor?'" she asked.

"It's not the person that matters. It's the sentiment, you stupid girl!" I snapped.

Jass looked as if I'd slapped her.

I felt embarrassed. This had been my failing, not hers.

"My apologies, Jass," I said. "Our place as mages is outside of non-magical society. While those in authority may ask for our assistance, we must not assume their authority for our own. Mundane, or non-magical, society must be allowed to develop and change without our interference.

"Do you understand this?" I asked.

"I think so," she said.

"That's good enough for now. If you have any questions, do not hesitate to ask them. The only stupid question," I began.

"Is one that is not asked," she said, completing my sentence.

"Just so, Jass," I said, smiling.

We ate in silence. Once we were nearly finished, Jass spoke.

"What is 'scrying?'" she asked.

"Scrying is a general term used to describe the use of magic to find things or people. It employs several forces and can be quite accurate. The enchantments I reinforced last night are to protect us from scrying by Marwoleth. You employ the Force of magic to shift, redirect or reflect any spells that may be cast to find you or something you wish to remain hidden.

"All mages put such enchantments, called scrywalls, on their abodes. It is not easy magic, but nearly all mages are capable of it, given enough practice. And the first step in learning to lay down scrywalls is to learn how scrying works," I said.

"That makes perfect sense. You must know how to do the thing before you can defeat the thing," Jass said.

"Excellent, Jass. Exactly right. The thing to remember about scrying is that the Force of magic must be carefully controlled and trained upon the object of the scry," I said. I looked up. Jass was staring at me with something like sadness in her eyes.

"Mandeight?" she asked.

"Yes," I answered.

"Did you sleep last night?" she asked.

"Some," I said. "I had to monitor the enchantments. I had to make sure this Marwoleth, or whoever has been enchanting stones here, wasn't doing what we're about to do."

"Should I make you some strong tea?" she asked.

"That's a good idea, lass. I'll need a pick-me-up," I said.

I drank the strong tea, and after half an hour, I was feeling a bit better.

"We will go to high ground. Scrying works best there. The mountain top near where we first met should be a suitable location," I announced as I grabbed my staff and prepared to depart.

Side-by-side, we climbed the trail leading to the mountain top. There was little vegetation here, but for low-lying weeds and scrub brush. The trail was narrow, likely only a game trail.

"Mandeight," Jass started.

"Yes," I said.

"Those rules you mentioned?" she started. "Why now?"

Her expression was grim.

"When I first went to the Collegium, long before they began teaching us about the Forces, and long before we were assigned mentors, they taught us our code of conduct. It was literally the first thing we learned," I answered.

I realized, a year or two after those classes, that they were not only teaching us the code by which we would live, but they were gauging our response to it. Unlike our later classes on the Forces, our earliest classes were more like discussions or conversations. Questions were encouraged. Discussion and arguments were common. All the while, the instructors were watching and listening. They were looking for apprentice mages who either couldn't or wouldn't understand the necessity of those rules. They were looking for potential dark mages.

Many students – nearly a quarter of them – were sent home after those first classes. For whatever reason, the instructors deemed those students unworthy to learn magic.

"But why were you so angry about it?" she asked, interrupting my train of thought.

"Marwoleth," I answered simply.

"You think I might be like him?" she asked quietly.

"Nothing of the sort. You seem to be a bright and good young lady, Jass. The constraints under which we live are not always things that people – even good people – will realize.

"Many of my classmates didn't make it past our classes on our code of conduct. They made fun of them. They scoffed at them. They didn't believe in their necessity. I'm sure Marwoleth was one of those students. Maybe they didn't even teach that stuff when he learned magic. I wanted to make sure you knew the rules," I said.

"I don't understand them all," she admitted.

"I know. Few of us do at first. That's why I want you to ask questions. Maybe I can help you understand why they're so important," I said.

We passed the switchback and the large rock where Jass and I first met. I tapped the boulder with my staff and looked at her with a wink.

She smiled at me.

We continued upward to the peak of the mountain.

"I love the view up here," she said, climbing further higher onto a boulder that jutted from the peak.

"It is a nice view, isn't it?" I said. Apart from the island below, one could see nothing but ocean as far as the eye could reach. It was a beautiful sight, but also isolating. Apart from the single city and a few farms below, there was no civilization in sight.

After we enjoyed the view for a long while, I set about to cast my scry spell.

"Scrying uses at minimum three Forces. The first is the Force of magic. We use this Force to create a connection between our focus, in this case, the stone, and our target, the one who enchanted it, the thing or person we are trying to find. Having something enchanted by this mage will make this much easier. This mage has left the essence of his magic, his power, his very personality upon this stone. It should be very easy to create a connection. It would only be easier if we had hair, fingernail clippings or something from the mage's body. But this stone should work well.

"Secondly, we must invoke the Force of earth for the stone. And finally, we shall invoke the Force of body to complete the connection to our mysterious mage," I said.

"So three Forces," she confirmed. "How do you use more than one at a time?"

"It is a very methodical process. I will first call the Force of magic, but I will hold it within my mind. Then I will call the Force of earth. Once called, I will let fly a portion of the magic Force, allowing it to attach itself to the stone. Once this connection is firmly established, I will call the Force of body, for the mage himself. Then I unleash the other portion of the magic Force and it will very briefly connect itself to our mage," I explained.

"Unleash? As in uncontrolled?" she asked. Clearly, she had been retaining what she read and copied from Xavier Birdstaff's book.

"Yes, Jass. Unleash. I shall exert no control over the magic Force. I will rely on the magic's connection to the stone and the body Force to direct the magic," I said.

"Isn't that dangerous? The book I'm copying says unleashing Forces is bad," she said. I smiled briefly. She was a good study. She would go far.

"Quite right. Unleashing a Force on its own almost always leads to disaster. But I shall release the other end of the magic Force upon the connection to the stone. The Forces of earth and body will create a conduit, a path, that the magic Force will follow naturally. It must follow it. It will be drawn to that connection," I explained.

"In fact," I continued, "the Force of magic must be unleashed. With scrying magic, that Force must have free reign, otherwise it won't find the connection. It's one of the few times it's safe to utterly let go of a summoned Force."

She nodded with a furrowed brow. I could almost see her cataloging this information in her mind for future reference.

I affixed a long leather cord to the stone and dangled it from my left hand. I closed my eyes and in my mind, I silently recited the rhyme of the Force of magic.

Then came the hard part. I was not well-versed in the Force of earth. Had I finished my training at the Collegium I wouldn't have had a problem, but I had been expelled.

"I need quiet, Jass. Earth magic is not my forte," I whispered. "Stand behind me, in case there's a ... problem."

I hear her step behind me. I spoke the rhyme of the Force of earth, a quatrain I had once learned. I didn't want to risk reciting it silently, as I didn't know it that well.

I was lucky. I felt the connection between my magic and the stone thrum into existence.

"Did you feel that, Jass?" I asked quickly.

"I think so," she said. "I can feel a band of heat between you and the stone."

"Very good," I said. "Now watch the stone."

I envisioned the symbol of the Force of body in my mind. Then I recited the rhyme of the Force of body aloud for Jass's sake.

My eyes were still closed when the unseen Force of body flew from my chest, carrying along with it the other end of the magic Force I summoned. It traveled along my arm, through the leather cord and into the stone. I felt the leather cord attempt to pull itself free. I tightened my grip to hold it.

"Do you see which direction the stone is pulling?" I asked Jass.

"I do!" she exclaimed. "It's pulling toward the East."

I opened my eyes and observed the stone.

"Shit!" I exclaimed.

"What is it?" Jass asked.

The stone and leather cord were now extended parallel to the ground, indicating a great distance. The stone was twitching and pulling toward the East, toward the Duchy of Eldemy.

"We have to go to the mainland," I said with reservation. "Whoever enchanted this stone is in Eldemy, or beyond."

"Why is that bad?" she said.

"I'm not exactly welcome in Eldemy," I replied. I looked down at the silver ring on the middle finger of my right hand. It had a small, nearly perfectly round stone, which many people mistook for a pearl. It showed a clear and pure white, which meant the person to which it was tied was very far away. That would change, and the stone would darken.

CHAPTER SIX

I needed to make arrangements before we could leave for Eldemy. I sought out my landlady and paid her three months' rent for my rooms, which she happily accepted.

My landlady, her name was Abigail Blackstone, was a young woman. Her father had been a pirate captain. Nearly eight years prior he was killed attempting to take a ducal ship headed south. The mission was successful, and the remaining crew dutifully brought Abigail her father's portion of the prize, or at least the portion they said was his.

This made Abigail Blackstone perhaps the richest woman on Ecota Isle. She used this money to purchase several properties, including my rooms and three other such homes. She also purchased the tavern and the restaurant across the street from where I lived, as well as a warehouse near the harbor.

Abigail Blackstone was a woman who knew how to turn her windfall into even more wealth, and that made her a very attractive woman to the men of Ecota Isle. She was also an intelligent woman and very pretty. Her hair was black, long and luxurious, gentle curls and waves framing her young, sun-kissed face. Her eyes were a deep, dark brown. She wore a bodice and skirts, attractively framing her young and fit body, but still maintaining modesty.

Had she been a woman of high birth, I suspected she would have the delicate, pale skin of a lady of leisure, contrasting with her dark hair and eyes, but the sun had tanned her face, neck and the portions of her bosom the bodice revealed.

In Eldemy, she would have been marked as a farm worker with that tan, but no one there would call her unattractive, even the most high-born lord.

I had been told that she had turned down no less than twenty proposals of marriage, including my own, but that had been after many hours of drinking and revelry with a pirate crew enjoying their shore leave.

Abigail stared at the dozen or so silver coins in her small, pretty hand

and frowned at me.

"Three months rent," she said. "Just where are you going?"

"I need to take a trip to the city of Eldemy. I have pressing business there. I'm not sure when I will return," I explained.

"What if you don't come back?" she asked.

"That's why I came here in person. I have many possessions in my rooms, some quite valuable. I was hoping I could compensate you to move them to someplace safe and store them until my return," I explained.

"I hope I will return within three months, but if I don't, I can pay you to store my possession. Indefinitely, I hope," I explained.

"How much to do that?" she asked. She had a reputation for having a good mind for business, and she was not shy about making sure she profited from each and every venture. She was hot.

"I happen to have three gold coins, struck in Eldemy itself. That should easily pay for laborers to move my possessions to your warehouse, and pay to keep them there for a year, or more. And there should be enough left to afford someone to watch over them at night," I said.

"I can hold them there for a year and six months, if that pleases you," she said.

"It would please me well, Mistress Blackstone," I said, smiling. "Should I return within three months, you can keep the gold coins and apply them toward my rents. Should I return after that, but before a year and six months hence, you may keep the balance for your trouble."

"That is a fair trade, Master Mandeight," she said. It was far more than a fair trade. It was extremely generous on my part, and she knew it.

"Very well," I said.

"Mandeight," she started, "why are you going to Eldemy?" There was concern in her voice, but only a little. She was very good at being, or at least seeming, concerned, and that was one of the most enchanting things about her. She had that intangible talent of making people, especially men, feel special and valued. It was a magic all its own.

"I have business there, but I may not return for some time. I'm not exactly welcome there, and I may be jailed, if the wrong people find me," I sighed.

"'Not welcome'" she repeated, "I thought you were banished. Told to never set foot there again."

"True, but the business to which I must attend is urgent and quite necessary," I said. "Should I not return within a year and six months, I would ask that you offer my possessions to Minister Graybeard. He is a good man and will allow me to buy them back at a fair price."

"I shall do such, Mandeight, though I hope you shall return before that is necessary," she said. While her words seemed kind, her tone was nothing but businesslike. This is why I had never proposed to Mistress Blackstone sober.

"So do I, Mistress Blackstone. So do I," I said.

It didn't take me long to find a ship bound for the city of Eldemy. It was called the Scarab. It was a ten-gun vessel, not overly large, but large enough for a comfortable journey. She had four rooms below decks, and I was able to secure one of them.

I met with the quartermaster, Jacob D'Jen, and paid him for passage for myself and my apprentice.

Jacob D'Jen was known to many of the inhabitants of Ecota Isle. Like most quartermasters, he had a good mind for numbers and logistics. He was a few inches shorter than I, so some might call him short. He had more weight on him than was healthy, but he carried it well. The hair on the top of his head was sparse, but what remained was brown and curly.

One might have called his face cherubic, but for several pock-mark scars that dotted his cheeks and nose. He was shirtless, which was common for sailors in this climate, and his breeches, no doubt taken from some ducal naval officer, were made from dark dyed velvet.

Over his left upper chest was the scar of a burn in the shape of a cross, so he had been captured and jailed once. If he were caught again with that scar, he would be dead, hanged as an unrepentant pirate.

Jacob was a serious man, like most quartermasters, as the mantle of authority weighed heavily on them. Unless in battle, the quartermaster, not the captain, was in charge of the ship. It was his duty to make sure the ship's stores were well-maintained, and he held the final word regarding where the ship was to sail and what prizes she would attempt to take.

The quartermaster was also responsible for distributing any treasure captured from a prize. In short, the quartermaster was the business manager of the ship, and the only time he wasn't in charge was during battle.

"I hear tell that you ain't wanted in Eldemy, master mage," Jacob said as I paid him.

"You have heard right, Jacob. I am not welcome in Eldemy. Why does everyone know my business?" I asked.

"Tis not a large city, master mage. Word travels," he said sheepishly.

"You know," he started reluctantly, "we might just get into hot water for even just taking you there."

I sighed. Everyone was getting their hands in my coin purse: first my landlady and now this quartermaster.

"I can pay a hazard fee if you feel it is necessary," I said reluctantly.

"No extra fee necessary, but I wonder if I might ask of you a favor, Master Mandeight," Jacob said slyly.

"What's that," I asked.

"Well, there's a vessel what makes a trip from near High Fall ruins to Eldemy and then on to Ecoja Smurt. Large ship. Few guns. She carries sundry wares: textiles, food and the like. Sometimes coin," Jacob started.

"And what does this have to do with me?" I asked.

"Well, we've been meaning to capture that ship as a prize. Seeing that we'll have a mage on board, that might even the odds if you get my meaning," he said. "And it would compensate for the risk of taking you where you ain't supposed to go."

I looked at Jacob flatly.

"I suppose I could provide some support," I said, feigning consideration. "But I would want something for that risk."

"If it's fair, I'll allow it," Jacob said, with the authority only a quartermaster could wield.

"First pick of the prize. Four items," I said.

"Three items. And I can deny them," he countered.

"Two items, and you don't get to deny them," I countered again.

"You can't have the ship," he said quickly.

"No intention of asking for it," I replied.

He spat in his left hand and extended it. I repeated the gesture and we shook on it. Pirates adopted the tradition of shaking with their left hands. Non-pirates insisted it was so they could stab each other in the back. I had no earthy idea if that was true or not, but I had known many pirates and engaged in business arrangements with them many times. I had never once been back-stabbed for my trouble.

"We leave on the morrow, before the second bell," Jacob said.

"When is the second bell?" I asked.

"Two hours past dawn. The first bell is rung at dawn, and it's rung every two hours thereafter," he explained patiently.

I nodded and left. I went back to my rooms to prepare for the voyage.

Jass was sitting at the supper table, going over her copy of the Xavier Birdstaff text. I walked into the library and selected two more small volumes to take on the voyage. One detailed the Force of magic, which was something all mages needed to learn. The second was a small volume on the Force of fire. While it hadn't helped me hone my skills, it might have been of use to Jass.

She looked up as I entered.

"What's the city of Eldemy like?" she asked.

"For you, I would use the term 'vast,'" I said. "This place here would be considered a hamlet compared to Eldemy. There are thousands of tradesmen of every kind: blacksmiths, tinkers, dressmakers, brewers, tanners, soap makers, butchers. You name the trade, and there will be a dozen plying it in the city of Eldemy.

"No one knows what the population is there, but it's probably a hundred times greater than here, maybe more. It's so big that only a small portion of the city is within the city walls, and that portion is five or six times larger than our city here. Craftsmen, farmers and the like have built their own homes and places of business outside of the city walls. There are probably ten times as many people living outside the walls than lived within."

She looked at me with disbelief.

"And you can get anything there," I continued. "This table right here came from Eldemy. The finest furniture makers in the duchy are in that city. Any kind of food you can think of is available there. Most things that weren't built here came from Eldemy. Hell, every ship that weighs anchor here in our port was built in that city."

"Whoa," she whispered.

I laughed.

"For someone who has only known an island life, the great city of

Eldemy will make your head spin, Jass," I went on. "But you have to keep your head. There are thieves, crooked shopkeepers, cutpurses and much worse. If it exists in this world, it exists in Eldemy."

Jass continued her studies as we ate our supper, which I paid for our landlady to send over.

"We have an early morning tomorrow. The Scarab leaves two hours past dawn. Go to bed, and I shall wake you at dawn," I said, standing to make my way to my own bed-chamber.

I had set a spell to wake me just before dawn, and I woke Jass soon thereafter.

Before we made our way to the Scarab, I said to Jass, "I need to place one more enchantment here. You may observe if you like, or you can go ahead to the Scarab."

She stayed, watching me intently.

The working took the better part of an hour, but in the end, it was successful.

"Whoa!" Jass exclaimed. "The door's gone," she shouted.

"Shh. Not so loud," I said, looking around, though there was no one yet on the walkways. "The door is still there, and anyone intimately familiar with these rooms will see it. The landlady, for example."

"But I live there and can't see it," she said.

"But you only lived here for a week or so. I've lived here for years," I explained. "It won't hold up to much scrutiny, but it is sufficient to stop any potential burglars."

"How long will it last?" she asked.

"Hard to say. Months, most likely. Perhaps a year," I said as I gathered our things together. "Let's go."

CHAPTER SEVEN

We were the only passengers booked aboard the Scarab. Most people on Ecota Isle either lived here or were visiting pirates. Few people actually traveled.

When we arrived at the dock, the Scarab had been transformed. She had been a place of chaos and clutter when I booked passage, but now everything was in its place.

Several crewmen sat ready up in the vessel's rigging. The clutter of barrels and crates that had scattered the deck was now stowed below. Even the deck had been scrubbed.

The crew was still shirtless, of course, except for the quartermaster, Jacob. He wore a vertically striped shirt of white and red, making him stand out among the crew.

As we arrived, he was barking orders, peppered with profanity.

Though I'd only been on ships a few times, I did know the protocol.

I stood at the bottom of the gangway and called up, "Permission to come aboard!"

Jacob looked startled, but gave the proper reply: "Permission granted."

"Master Mandeight. Welcome aboard," Jacob said in greeting once we were on the deck. "This must be your apprentice."

"Yes, this is my apprentice, Jass. Jass, this is Jacob D'Jen, quartermaster of the Scarab," I said by way of introduction.

"Pleased to meet you, Master D'Jen," Jass said formally. It was strange that a girl who'd spent so much time eking out a most humble and modest existence on the most distant of the Far

Isles would be so well versed in such formality. I was starting to wonder if she might have been high-born.

Jacob personally showed us to our cabin, which was small, though it had a bunk bed. There was a small writing desk and a single chair, and that was the extent of our amenities.

The first week of our voyage aboard the Scarab was uneventful and pleasant. The cook, whom I was told was "rescued" from a ship of the Duke's fleet, was very talented. He insisted that Jacob, as quartermaster, maintain a supply of spices and seasonings, and everyone was grateful for it.

We ate few of the provisions Jacob had brought on board, as I was able to coax fish close to the water's surface using a combination of the water and body Forces, and the crew happily caught them. As a result, we had fresh fish for most evening meals. I was able to coax a sea turtle to the surface one evening, but the crew refused to bring it aboard. They said it was bad luck to eat a sea turtle while at sea.

Even the breakfast porridge was a delight. The cook seasoned it was dried salted pork and a few other spices he refused to divulge.

On the eighth day, there was a knock at our cabin door. It was Kidal, the tall, dark-skinned gunnery master. He was nearly a head taller than I. He had a broad, scarred chest. Like the rest of the crew, he eschewed the use of shirts. His scars were ragged and savage, and each must have been an excruciating ordeal.

This was a man of labor. His arms were thick and tight with muscle, and the sight of his chest would have made any high-born lady swoon. The hair on his head was black and tightly curled, though cropped short, as is the fashion with most sailors. His face was unshaven, though I suspected he'd shaved on his last night ashore on Ecota Isle.

His eyes were dark and serious, and he walked with the kind of authority that would make most men follow him.

"Ah, Master Kidal, come in. To what do we owe the pleasure," I said with irony. Kidal had not spoken more than eight words to me on the voyage so far, and most of the time that was, 'move,' or 'go away.'

"Come on deck," he said and turned and walked away. He had the accent of a southerner, someone from the regions far south of the ruins of High Fall.

I shrugged at Jass and motioned for her to follow me. She got up from the little writing desk in our stateroom. She had long finished copying her first text and was now ready to begin some rudimentary callings, but I was going to wait until we were on land. Having an apprentice mage experiment on a ship in the middle of the ocean was unwise.

To keep her mind occupied, I'd presented her with a text on the Force of magic, "Magicum and Its Uses," by Tedor Crummen. The original text was more than a century old, but it was by far the best treatise on the Force of magic.

When we emerged from below, I saw Kidal climbing the ladder to the aft deck, so we followed.

There standing before us was the captain, who I had not even seen on the voyage thus far, though I knew him by reputation.

Kidal gave him a nod and a salute, and said, "Captain."

"Master Mandeight, and Apprentice Jass, come up, please," the captain said.

"I am Captain Nicholas Tallor. Welcome aboard. A bit late for welcomes, but my time has been consumed with other matters, so my apologies," he said with a deep, lyric voice.

Unlike the rest of the crew, he wore a shirt, and over that a black and blue doublet. This was no captured garment. It was made for Captain Tallor, as there were no cuts nor slashes on it, and it fit him well.

He was about my height, my height being average, and he had a serious face, much like most quartermasters I'd met. His head was clean-shaven, and he had a short but well-groomed gray beard.

When he spoke, I wondered if he had once been an officer in the Duke's navy. That's where many pirate captains came from. Because pirate captains only took command during combat, they had to be well-versed in naval tactics, and the only people who learned that were naval captains. I wonder what had made this naval officer turn to a life of piracy.

"No need, Captain Tallor. It is a pleasure. I know you by reputation. That's why I sought out your vessel," I replied. That wasn't entirely untrue. I'd heard he was a competent captain, but I was just looking for the next ship leaving for Eldemy.

"That's very kind of you, master mage," he said. "You know our gunnery master, Kidal."

"Yes. We've had many a pleasant conversation," I said.

Kidal scowled, and the captain smiled.

"Indeed," he said with a wink. "We are within sight of Tremble Isle. Just on the horizon to the larboard."

"Which one is that?" I asked.

"The left," he explained patiently. I looked to the left of the bow and could see a small jagged shape silhouetted by the morning sun.

"We shall lie in wait in the harbor there. That will conceal us as the prize approaches," he said. He then gestured to a small table behind the helm. We walked to it, and there lay a detailed map of the sea to the west of Eldemy. It was under a pane of perfectly formed glass, which was set into a wooden frame with hinges on one side and a hasp on the other.

The map showed the island, and I could clearly make out the harbor he'd mentioned.

"She's still at least a day out, but Kidal can fill you in on the details. Then you can suggest what your part in this venture might be," he said cautiously.

"We've never worked with a mage before, so we're not quite

sure what you're capable of," he said, looking hard at Kidal. "Kidal, tell him what he needs to know."

Kidal nodded. The captain excused himself and returned to the helm, where another crewman I hadn't even noticed guided the Scarab.

Kidal didn't even really acknowledge my existence when he began speaking.

"She'll approach from the North, usually on the eastern side of the isle," he started. "She'll be at full sail when she makes her tack into the harbor, then they'll strike sails. They use their momentum to get into the harbor. It's small and hard to navigate at speed."

"Is that where the attack will take place?" I asked.

"No attack!" he said sternly. "We'll be at the eastern edge of the harbor. She won't see us on account of the terrain. Then we'll raise our colors and hail them with a lantern."

"You won't fire immediately?" I asked.

Kidal looked at me coldly. "No, we won't. Cannon damages cargo, kills hostages, sinks ships. We only do that if they choose to run. Or fight, which they seldom do, if we're doing our job right," he explained.

"Right. Warn them first. So what's my part?" I asked.

"That depends on what you can do, mage," he said. He'd used the word 'mage' as if it was a curse. That offended me.

"Well, I'm good with air and water. And the mind," I said ominously.

Before I knew it, Kidal held a dagger at my throat. His dark eyes narrowed.

"You try it, mage, and I'll slit your throat," he growled.

"Kidal!" I heard the captain say. Kidal withdrew the dagger with a dark scowl, but he didn't sheath it.

"Can you turn the bow ship toward the West? That'll put her

facing the westerly winds. Even if she gets her sails up, she won't be able to maneuver much, and that takes her larboard cannons out of play," he said.

"Yes, I can do that. I'll need to be on the water to create that much force. I'll need a small boat or something. And we'll need to lash it somehow to the Scarab, on the side facing the prize," I said.

He frowned. "Why is that?"

"Well," I began, "I'll be, for lack of a better term, pushing the water at the bow of the prize. Without something substantial at my back, the water that displaces that water I push will just push me in the opposite direction. That will make it much harder to maintain the spell long enough to turn the prize."

I saw his eyes narrow as he began to understand the mechanics of what I was going to do.

Finally, he said, "I see. We can arrange to lash the launch to the side. I'll get the carpenters working on it."

"Thank you," I said. Clearly, Kidal didn't like me, so I figured being polite might change that, at least in some small way.

"But that will also put you in the line of fire, should there be such an exchange," he added with a menacing grin.

Only once before had I been on a ship during a sea battle. It was, and I do not say this lightly, the most terrifying experience of my life. I couldn't imagine experiencing that on a little rowboat stuck beneath the gun ports on the fighting side of the ship.

"That doesn't sound pleasant," I said. Kidal smiled.

"But I see no other choice," I added. Kidal's smile was replaced with an expression of confusion, which lasted only a moment and was quickly replaced with cold contempt.

Once we concluded our planning, Jass and I left the bridge.

That evening, while in our stateroom, I heard Jass get up and leave. It certainly wasn't yet time, as I could feel the bucking motion of the ship as it sailed toward the harbor of Tremble

Isle.

I waited until her footsteps faded away and quietly got up to follow her.

I was a step or two from emerging on the deck of the Scarab when I heard her voice and the deep voice of a man. It was Kidal.

"Why are you up?" I heard him ask Jass.

"I wanted to ask you a question, Master Kidal," she said with trepidation.

"About the plan? Is there a problem?" he asked.

"No. Not that. I wanted to know what happened between you and Mandeight. Why there is bad blood? Why you hate him so?" she asked. I was surprised. I'd clearly sensed his disdain for me, but hadn't wonder much about it. There were more pressing matters.

"I do not hate him," Kidal replied.

"But you put a blade to his throat. You clearly revel in the fact that this plan will put him in danger. Why?" she pressed.

There was a long silence, and I thought about peeking on to the deck to see if I could get a glimpse of his expression, but I chose to remain hidden.

"I have only known a few mages in my days, young miss, and I must say, such encounters have been less than pleasant," he said.

"But you only just met Master Mandeight?" she said.

"True, but he strikes me as typical of his sort," he replied.

"He is the only mage I've ever met," she admitted. "But I don't understand."

I heard him sigh, and it sounded like he sat down on something. I quietly sat down on the stairs, as this was going to be a long conversation, and I wanted to hear it.

Yes, I know eavesdropping is rude, but I was about to go into a dangerous situation with this man, and I wanted to see where I stood.

"I was born in a land far from here, young miss," he started. I had to stifle a sigh. This was going to be a very long conversation.

"When I was young – much younger than you are now – a mage from Eldemy came to our city. My father was an armorer, and this mage needed repairs to his retainers' armor. There had been a fight, and their armor needed mending.

"I was there watching. And my father gave him a price. The mage said it was too high and tried to haggle the price down, but the price my father offered was fair. I knew that much, even as a child," Kidal said.

"The mage then threatened my father, saying he would do terrible things if he did not do it for less. My father refused and told the mage to do his worst. Then the mage asked if he could do a cheaper repair, not take as much time or use cheaper material," he continued.

"My father said he could, but the armor would not be strong, that it might be too brittle and the repairs might shatter in battle. The mage said that was fine with him.

"After he left, my father said, 'never trust a man who does not respect those who protect his life, for his life means more to him than anything else. This is the sign of a coward,'" Kidal concluded.

"But that was just one mage. Surely it isn't fair to judge all by the actions of one," she said.

"That is both true and wise, young miss, but I have met other mages. I have met several, in fact, and each has been more concerned with their own well-being than anything else," Kidal said.

"In fact," he continued, "each has been selfish and proud. Each has been greedy and deceptive. I have been swindled by many mages. I even worked for one as his bodyguard, and saw for myself how little they care for those who serve them, no matter how loyal."

"Well, Mandeight is proud, to be sure," Jass mused. I frowned. How dare she!

"But," she continued, "he is very generous. He took me in. He clothed me. He feeds me. He put a roof over my head."

"And what does he ask in return?" Kidal asked with suspicion.

"Nothing like that!" she exclaimed.

"Oh," Kidal said with surprise. "Then how do you repay him?"

"I cook for him. I clean, sometimes. Mostly he makes me study. He's got me copying books. He says that's the best way for me to learn," she said.

"And when he weaves his magic, he explains to me what he's doing, and how and why. He gives me so much: food, shelter, knowledge, and asks for very little in return. That seems neither greedy nor selfish," she concluded.

"Perhaps you are right, young miss, or perhaps mages treat their students better than others. Perhaps they fear you may one day hex him if he doesn't treat you well," Kidal countered.

"Perhaps, but from all I've seen he is a kind and generous man," she said.

I felt a pang of guilt. It was clear that I was not as good of a man as she thought I was. When I brought her in, I was thinking more about the prospects of a free housemaid than teaching her.

"We shall see what he is made of later tonight," Kidal countered.

"I think we shall," she said quietly.

"I do not hold such disdain for you, young miss," he hastened to say. "I hope that once you become fully trained you remain the way you are. You certainly show loyalty and compassion. And bravery."

"Bravery?" she asked.

"Oh yes. There are not many young girls who would confront a scary pirate to defend her teacher," he growled.

"You don't seem that scary to me," she replied.

I stifled a laugh.

"Get to bed! I have much to prepare." And with that, he stalked away.

I rushed as quietly as I could back to our room, but I wasn't quite quick enough. Jass opened the door before I could crawl back into bed.

"Master Mandeight, you're up," she said, startled.

"Oh yes," I stammered. "I was wondering where you got off it. It's time to begin preparations."

"What kind of preparations?" she asked.

"Not so much preparations," I lied, "but I want you to understand what I'm going to do and how I'm going to do it."

She sat on her bed and looked at me intently. She would make a good apprentice, perhaps better than I deserved, which quickly became clear.

After I explained the mechanics of the spell I was going to use to turn the prize away from us, rendering its cannons useless, Jass asked me an uncomfortable question.

"Master Mandeight," she started, "you're about to use the art to help these pirates to take and loot that ship. How does that fit with the code of conduct of the Collegium?" she asked.

Damn it, I thought. This was not the kind of ethical question I wanted to answer right now.

Here's the thing: I needed to get to Eldemy. There was a dark mage there who was kidnapping people, and after our research, we discovered it was very likely Marwoleth the necromancer. The very same necromancer who tried to usurp the Duke of Eldemy, who tried to take over the only great nation I knew.

This was a time when the ends justified the means, and the Collegium code didn't have much room for that.

"You need to look at proportions, Jass," I started. "Using the art to help a pirate ship capture another ship is wrong, certainly.

But why are we doing it?"

"To find and defeat Marwoleth," she said, somewhat crestfallen.

"Exactly. Which is the greater wrong? Helping these pirates capture a ship? Or Marwoleth doing whatever he has planned?" I asked.

"Marwoleth," she said. "Who knows what he has planned? He's already taken my mother." I winced. He hadn't just taken Jass's mother, he'd very likely turned her into a soldier in his undead army, if history was any indication.

"Just so, Jass," I said. "And if we have to break a few rules to get to him, isn't it worth it?"

"I guess so," she started. Then she showed something I had not seen in her before. I had seen kindness and empathy, but I had not seen this: morality.

"If we break the rules that make us better than him," she said, "are we really better than him?"

Damn this girl and her insight, I thought.

"Your observation is certainly true on some level," I sighed. "Following the code is one thing that distinguishes us from Marwoleth, but there are even more important differences," I said.

"Such as?" she asked, eying me cautiously.

"Marwoleth is using his magic to heinous ends. It's not simply helping pirates steal things, it's perverting life itself. That cannot stand," I said.

She thought about this for a while. I watched her as she reasoned out our conundrum.

"I suppose that's an even more important difference between Marwoleth and us," she said.

CHAPTER EIGHT

It was a moonless night as the Scarab sat nearly motionless in the Tremble Isle harbor. The crew was speaking in whispers, for there was an entire town on the shore, and our presence was to be a secret. The captain had explained that if the townsfolk knew we were there, they might try to alert our quarry, and we would have no way to stop them.

I climbed down the rope ladder to the small launch which had been secured to the Scarab with ropes fished through the gun ports. I'd hoped that the carpenters would affix cleats to the side of the Scarab that I could untie, should things turn violent, but that was not to be.

I felt the rope ladder jostling, and looked up. Jass was beginning her climb down.

"What are you doing?" I demanded.

"I'm going on the launch," she said simply.

I noticed Kidal's dark face peering through one of the cannon ports. He craned his head to look up at Jass.

"You most certainly are not," I said.

"I want to see you cast the spell," she said. "And you might need my help," she added.

"I most certainly won't need your help," I replied. "Besides, it's too dangerous. If things get violent, you'll be right in the line of fire."

"But," she started.

"Absolutely not," I said, with great magely finality.

"He's right, young miss," Kidal added. "Leave your master to his fate. You can always find another teacher." Then he let out a great basso laugh.

Jass scowled at me, then at Kidal. Then, to my surprise, she continued climbing down to the launch.

Kidal reached out with a long, muscular arm and grabbed her by the wrist. He began pulling her through the cannon port.

Then Jass reached over and bit his arm.

Kidal grimaced in pain.

"Jass!" I shouted. "Kidal is an officer on this vessel! He is well within his rights to have you flogged for assaulting him!"

As I spoke, Kidal twisted his arm around, freeing it from her teeth and began pulling her through the cannon port.

"Don't worry, mage. She's coming with me," Kidal said though the pain.

She shouted and beat on him as she disappeared through the cannon port. Then his face reemerged.

"Clap her in irons if you have to," I shouted.

Kidal answered me with a toothy grin.

It was difficult to see the prize silently drift into the harbor without the light of the moons, but I could make out its vague shape none the less. The Scarab's starboard cannons were loaded and ready, the cannon crews peering through the ports with curiosity.

As I began calling the Force of water, the launch rocked violently, and I looked around to find Jass standing next to me.

"Damn it, Jass!" I whispered through gritted teeth.

"I want to see," she said.

There was no time to argue, as the prize was about to pass us. I shoved her down and said, "shut up and stay there." She sat quietly, with not so much as a frown. Her face showed excitement and curiosity.

I looked up at the port behind me and saw Kidal. He was scowling at her, raising his fist.

I called the Force of water. I silently recited the rhyme, rather than just summoning the Force, as this working would require great power. I raised both hands over my head, and the water before me rose nearly twenty feet in the air.

I heard Jass whisper, "whoa!"

Then with a downward gesture, I pushed the mass of water away from me, just ahead of the bow of our quarry.

The massive wave rushed toward the prize, leaving a large "pit" in the water before us. The launch began to lurch into the pit as water rushed in to fill the void.

The momentum of the water continued and it slammed the launch against the side of the Scarab. The sound was almost deafening.

It was so loud that someone aboard the prize heard it.

Though the prize was now turning away from us, propelled by the wave, the aft-most cannon on the prize's larboard side fired.

With that brief flash, I could tell the cannonball was coming straight for us. I raised my hands and unleashed the Forces of air and bolstering. The air before us turned as solid as stone. I looked up as the spark-strewn cannonball flew above me.

The last thing I saw was the cannonball stopping a few feet from Kidal's wide-eyed face. My head slammed against the Scarab. Everything went black.

CHAPTER NINE

I felt bitter cold and an intense, searing pain.

"I have mended the strand," a beautiful female voice said.

"But will it hold?" another voice, this of perhaps a young male, said.

"It will hold," the woman replied.

"But the flesh has been harmed," the man said.

"It will heal," the woman said.

I tried to speak, but I couldn't. I didn't recognize either voice.

There was white light, and the feeling of pain and cold grew far worse. I wondered if I was hallucinating, or dead.

"Mandeight?" someone said.

I could hear moaning, and it made the pain, which I now realized was in my head, intolerable. It felt like a thousand white-hot needles piercing the back of my skull, deep into my brain.

"Mandeight!" the voice repeated.

I realized the moaning was coming from me. I made an effort to stop moaning, and the pain lessened only slightly. The needles in my brain were now only red-hot, I supposed.

I opened my eyes and quickly closed them again. The sky was so bright, it burned my eyes and set my whole body on fire with pain.

"You hit your head, Mandeight. The surgeon says you have to wake up now, or you may never wake up," the voice said tearfully. I realized it was Jass.

"What happened," I said, but I don't think Jass understood me.

"Master Oler! Master Oler! He's speaking," she shouted with a piercing voice that sent me reeling.

I felt more than heard heavy footsteps approach.

"I'm here! I'm here, lass," an old man's voice said. He had a northern accent, from Ecoja Smurt, or somewhere thereabouts.

"Master Mandeight! Are you awake?" the old voice said.

"I fought someone in Ecoja Smurt once. I hope it wasn't you," I quipped.

"What's he saying about sweet rolls?" Jass said with confusion and concern.

"Tis nothing to worry about, Jass. His words are just mixed up. Bound to happen with such a blow to the head," the old man said. "Let's get him below where it's darker. Kidal! A hand, if you please."

The searing pain in my head turned to throbbing as I was jostled and manhandled below deck. They carried me using a sheet of canvass or perhaps a piece of sail. Once settled, I again risked opening my eyes. It wasn't as painful this time around.

The first thing I saw was the suntanned, wrinkled face of the ship's surgeon, Master Oler. His spectacles were perched low on his nose, and his head was tilted back as he looked me in the eyes. His nose was large and red, probably from too many dips into the rum barrel. His bald head was marked with burns and spots from too much sun.

"He's definitely concussed, but that he's awake is a good sign," Oler said reassuringly. "You've taken a blow to the head, Master Mandeight," he said very loudly, the way surgeons talk to their patients. "Quite a serious one, so we can't have you lying down for too long. I need you to sit up, if you can."

I tried to sit upright, but the table spun and whirled, and I slumped back down.

"Don't just stand there gawking, you two. Help him up!" he said. Small gentle hands took my left arm while strong hands took my right. They pulled me upright. To my surprise, the larger, stronger hands were more gentle.

The old surgeon held up a finger. "Now follow my finger as best you can," he said. I did.

"Very good, Master Mandeight. Very good," he exclaimed. "He doesn't seem too badly off. He'll be right as rain in a week or two, I suspect."

It was then that I realized we were in the middle of a ship battle. I tried to get up, saying, "the fight!"

"What's he saying?" Jass asked again.

"Never mind that, Jass. It'll pass in a day or so. He'll be ordering you around in no time," the surgeon answered.

In fact, it wasn't until the second day that I realized the words I was intending to speak were different than the words I heard myself speak, and it was yet another day before anyone could understand me.

"I've never treated a mage before, Master Mandeight, but I suggest you not attempt any magic until you're well-healed," the surgeon, Oler, said when he checked up on me.

"And when will that be?" I asked.

"Can't say for certain, and I don't pretend to know how magic works, but I would suggest waiting until you can walk on your own and when the pain is gone," he answered.

"What happened with the prize?" I asked.

"We took her," said Kidal's basso voice from behind me. I breathed a sigh of relief.

"Had you not taken care of that stray shot I dare say it would have caused chaos with the cannon crew. They might have come about and done us in," he said.

"Casualties?" I asked.

"None," he said. "On our side at least," he added with a smile in his voice.

"How did they see us? How did they know to fire?" I asked.

"They had a mage of their own, it seems. He was killed with our first barrage," Kidal said. "The captain and quartermaster want to have a word with you when you feel up to it." He stalked away and climbed the stairs to the deck.

"Kidal is still a ray of sunshine, I see," I quipped.

"He's tired. He's been sitting here with you and Jass when not on duty. He hasn't slept since we took the prize," the surgeon said. "He won't say what happened, but he seems to think he owes you a debt."

I frowned. I didn't remember what had happened and wouldn't for another day or two.

"Where's Jass?" I asked.

"She's in your quarters, asleep. I told her if she didn't get some rest, I would have her locked in the brig," Oler said.

I smiled but didn't risk even a chuckle, for fear it might worsen my headache.

The next morning Jass helped me up to the deck to seek out the captain and the quartermaster. They were both in the captain's quarters, just below the bridge. The room was filled with books and treasures and trinkets, no doubt some of the spoils from the prize.

There was a desk in the room that was grand enough for a member of the duke's privy council. It was constructed of a dark brown wood except for the large front panels, which were of a lighter wood and carved with various coats of arm and sigils I recognized from my days in Eldemy, though I couldn't place them. It, like every other horizontal surface in the quarters was stacked with goods from the prize.

The desk was also large enough to use as a bed, possibly for two.

Captain Tallor sat behind the desk, and Quartermaster Jacob sat in an ornate chair at the front of it. They seemed to be taking inventory of their treasures, as the captain was examining a vase or pitcher, and Jacob was furiously scribbling in a ledger.

I cleared my throat as we entered.

"Ah, Master Mandeight! It's good to see you up and among the living," Jacob the quartermaster said. He didn't get up, but he offered a very broad and genuine smile as a welcome.

Captain Tallor got up from behind the comically enormous desk and approached me with a somber expression on his face. As he approached, he extended his left hand. I took it, and we shook.

"I wanted to personally thank you, Mandeight. Were it not for your actions, the day certainly would not have been ours. I dare say we would all be prisoners, or dead," he said seriously.

"Of course. I'm just glad I could help," I replied, a bit flummoxed.

"I do not know if you've been made aware, but our prize, a galleon called the Duchess Adina, had a mage of their own. He must have caught sight of us as their vessel began to turn. The crew and I owe you a great debt of gratitude," he said with a brief smile. His smile was short and insincere, but the grave look in his eyes told me he was speaking the truth.

Then he turned to Jacob and said, "Well, I'll leave you to it," and he walked out onto the deck.

Jacob was still sitting in front of the desk, still writing furiously.

"There's the matter of your prize, Master Mandeight. Captain Tallor suggested, and I agreed, that you should have the pick of the prize, without limit," Jacob said as he finished up whatever he was writing. It's a hell of a mental feat to write one thing while you're speaking another. Most people can't do it, and when they can, they usually write and speak slowly, sort of taking turns with each task. The quartermaster did both seemingly at full speed.

I realized Jacob D'Jen had a sharp mind, far more than he had let on earlier.

"Since you were incapacitated, and we couldn't offer you the

Duchess Adina, as she had to be scuttled, I left it to your apprentice, Jass, to decide what that would be," he said.

I winced but tried to conceal it.

"That is kind of you. And what did she select?" I asked, almost not wanting to know the answer.

He looked at me apologetically and said, "well, I wasn't sure it was the sort of thing you would have picked, but your apprentice said it had ... certain properties. We suggested several other items, but she was rather insistent."

He walked to the corner of the room, where a large item, more than six feet tall, was covered by a section of sailcloth. He removed the sailcloth, revealing a large oval mirror with an ornate filigree frame and stand. To the right of the mirror, about midway up its height was a small brass cup affixed to the frame.

I looked at the mirror. The surface was bright, polished and flawless. Such mirrors were extremely rare. Most mirrors had waves and other imperfections that at least slightly distorted the reflected image, but not this mirror. I looked at my reflection, and it was literally perfect.

I turned my eye to the mirror's frame and stand. The mirror and frame were oval in shape, and the frame appeared to be made of hammered brass, polished to a finish almost as reflective as the mirror.

"There's also this," he said, walking to a table, where sat a small wooden chest. He opened it, revealing eight small glass orbs. I stepped away from the mirror and examined the contents of the chest. Each of the eight orbs contained what appeared to be shifting and swirling smoke of differing colors as if I could see the enchantments without having to summon a Force, which I didn't want to risk in my current state.

"I could sense the spells upon them, Master Mandeight," Jass said with hopeful pride.

"Indeed, you did, Jass. Indeed, you did," I muttered as I approached the mirror once again.

The brass was covered with intricate etchings, some pictographs, some of an ancient language with which I was somewhat familiar.

"You have done well," I whispered.

I caught a glimpse of Jacob in the mirror, and he was frowning. No doubt he assumed the girl would pick something fanciful and useless, but by my reaction, he realized she might have picked the most valuable item on the Duchess Adina.

"This mirror dates back to the days of the Old Empire," I said. "This is the old Eldemic script. It must be ten thousand years old, or more."

"Do you know what it does?" Jass asked excitedly.

"I have no idea," I said with distracted wonder.

"I picked that chest with the globes, as well," she added. "There are spells on them as well."

I examined the orbs again. The colored smoke within each reminded me of an artistic representation of the intricate lines of enchantments when I use the Force of magic to look upon them.

"I dare say that mirror and these orbs make a set," I said. Jass sat down in a chair with a satisfied smile. She glanced over at Jacob with a triumphantly raised eyebrow, but Jacob avoided eye contact with her.

"Tell me, quartermaster," I began, "can I ask of you one more favor since I am owed such a debt?" I asked.

"Ask it," Jacob said. There was no reluctance in his voice. Captain Tallor's words of an owed debt must have rung with a note of truth, even to the quartermaster.

"Will we pass by Lovers' Isle on our way to Eldemy? I should like to store this in my cottage there," I asked.

"That is not out of our way, assuming the stop won't take too long," Jacob answered.

"It should only take a couple hours, and I would be most appreciative," I replied. "And I would consider it a debt paid," I added.

"Very well, Master Mandeight. I will set course for Lovers' Isle," he said, leaving the cabin for the bridge.

That evening Jass and I sat atop the forecastle, enjoying the darkening view of the open sea as the sun gradually set in the West. We had just finished our dinner, which consisted of roasted salt pork, braised carrots with honey and a generous portion of a very delicate grain with which I was unfamiliar. All of it had been captured from the Duchess Adina. Clearly, the Duchess Adina had stores fine enough for the highest nobility, and the Scarab's cook was more than up to the challenge of turning these stores into an incredible meal.

I sat back, my belly full and my headache fading, and looked toward the stern. Many of the crew sat on the deck eating, and to my surprise I saw Captain Tallor with them, sitting on a small barrel, exchanging no-doubt bawdy stories with the crew, judging by their guffaws and similar reactions.

"Is that mirror really ten thousand years old?" Jass asked.

"At least," I said. "It could be far older. The Old Empire extended back to the beginning of recorded history. It could be as much as twenty thousand years old, I would guess."

"What happened to it? The Old Empire, I mean," she asked.

"That is a complicated question, and I suspect you'd get a different answer from every historian you asked," I said.

"The dates we use today count the years from the death of the last emperor. Some say he left no clear heir. Others say the heir was challenged because he was too young or incompetent. Whatever the reason, the Old Empire just sort of dissolved.

"You realize the Duke of Eldemy should by all rights be called a king, yes?" I said. Jass just shrugged, her long, red hair shifting with the gesture. "The title of Duke of Eldemy dates back before the fall of the Old Empire, in fact. Back then, the duke was but a vassal to the emperor, though no doubt a powerful one. Duke

Elkis the 434th, or whatever the number is, and his predecessors before him kept the title out of tradition, most likely.

"It's said that the Old Empire extended to the tundras to the North, to the South for ten thousand leagues beyond High Fall and to the West past the Wall Mountains and the Sea of Sand. No doubt there were countless duchies, earldoms and counties that made up the empire. The land we know as Eldemy was but one small part of a very grand whole," I said.

"Where was the capital?" she asked.

"No one knows," I said. "Historical records of the Old Empire are quite literally falling apart with age, and even when we find whole pages, the language has changed so much that we can hardly read it. I once tried to teach myself Old Eldemic, not very successfully, but my efforts allowed me to at least recognize the writing on the mirror frame."

"You don't have any idea what it does?" she asked.

"None whatsoever," I said. "Once our current task is completed, we can set to figuring that out. Until then, I'll store it in my cottage on Lovers' Isle."

"Will it be safe there?" she asked.

"Safe enough. Lovers' Isle is all but uninhabited, and my cottage is very well-concealed. I should like to store it in my rooms on Ecota Isle, but that's hardly workable now, and we dare not travel with it in Eldemy. I wouldn't want to risk damaging it, or having it stolen," I said.

"Why do you think it was on that ship?" Jass asked.

"I don't know, though I suspect it was the property of the mage on the Duchess Adina. Did you happen to hear the mage's name?" I asked.

"I heard one of the Duchess Adina's crew call him Basma," she said.

I dropped my fork onto my nearly empty plate, and it fell to the deck.

"Basma? Are you quite sure?" I asked. The name was familiar to me, and I was hoping she was wrong.

"Yeah. I think so. Kidal was there. He heard it too. He can confirm if I heard it right," she said. She gestured with her head to the aft of the Scarab, and I turned to see Kidal approaching.

Kidal walked through a maze of dining crewmen, and he only paused in his travels to give Captain Tallor a reverent salute as he passed. He carried two cups. As he approached the forecastle, he handed me one and hopped up to sit on a barrel. The cup was filled with a brown ale. I took a sip, it was cool and refreshing. It was only slightly bitter, with a rich, malty body.

"Thank you, Master Kidal," I said, raising my cup. He raised his in return and drank. I noted that he looked me in the eye as we toasted, but not with hatred or disdain. His expression was neutral and serious. Then he let out a great yawn.

"Just call me Kidal. We have been in battle together, and you conducted yourself well, mage. No need for formalities," he said with a slight and tired smile.

I felt my eyebrows raise in surprise. Kidal smiled wanly again.

"I heard you take my name in vain," he said to Jass with a teasing tone.

"I was only saying that you heard the name of the mage on the Duchess Adina," Jass explained.

"Yes. It was Basma. The crew made quite a noise about his death. The captain was practically in tears," Kidal spat with a laugh.

"As well they should," I muttered.

"Why is that?" Kidal asked.

"Basma is, or should I say was, one of the Cardinal Mages," I said.

They both looked at me with confusion, so I continued.

"The Duke of Eldemy has four mages who act as viziers, along with his non-mage viziers. The viziers are his counsel and advisors. Each Cardinal Mage is named for a cardinal direction on a compass.

"It's been some time since I received any political news from Eldemy, but Basma was the Cardinal Mage of the South," I said.

"The Duke has four mages at his disposal?" Kidal asked, sounding impressed.

"Yes, quite so. Each Cardinal Mage is responsible for certain aspects of the ruling of Eldemy. The Cardinal Mage of the South represents fire. He is, or was, primarily a war mage," I said, turning to Kidal.

"We're quite fortunate that he was killed in the first barrage," I said. "Had he survived it, we wouldn't be here now, though we might be having a nice conversation in the afterlife."

Kidal bowed his head in relief, saying, "that's why I hate mages. You never know if you're dealing with a dangerous one or one like you."

Jass gasped.

I looked at Kidal, and his face was expressionless except for his eyes, which were trying not to betray the jest he'd just said. Clearly, he was ribbing me, which was an improvement from the hateful disdain I'd experienced before.

I winked at him, and the smile in his eyes slowly spread across his dark face. He let out a hearty laugh.

"Who are the others?" Jass asked.

"Huh," I replied, not having heard the question.

"Who are the other Cardinal Mages," Jass pressed.

"Well, there's Gazar, Cardinal Mage of the North. He is responsible for both agriculture and defense. He's a very capable nature mage, and a savant when it comes to concealment magic. Then there's Samana, the Cardinal Mage of the East. She is responsible for intelligence, spying and scrying. I actually went to school with her: quite bright. And you are already familiar with the Cardinal Mage of the West, Jass," I said.

"I am?" she asked.

"Yes. Xavier. Xavier Birdstaff," I said. "He is responsible for internal security and the personal security of the Duke."

"He's the author of that book on Forces?" she said, though it wasn't really a question. "I'd assumed he was dead."

"Unfortunately not," I replied. "He will be a major concern once we're in Eldemy, though I must say, Samana now concerns me as well. Once it is known that Basma is dead or missing, she'll attempt to find him, and that mirror may lead her to us."

Kidal went wide-eyed. "We should pitch it over the side," he said.

"You will do no such thing," I said, laughing. "They won't know he's missing for days or a week at least. But it does underline the urgency of getting the mirror to Lovers' Isle. I have sufficient defenses there to shield it, and I can reinforce them before we depart."

"We should hasten our journey there," Kidal said, standing up. "I'll inform the quartermaster." He walked away. He stormed past Captain Tallor and the rest of the crew and made his way to the bridge. I saw him whispering with Jacob D'Jen.

A few moments later, I heard Kidal bark orders to the crew. About half of the crew sitting with the captain jumped into action. They climbed the rigging and began adjusting the sails. Soon the Scarab lurched to the side as our speed increased.

"Why will the Cardinal Mages work against us? Wouldn't they want to stop this Marwoleth? This necromancer?" Jass asked.

"Oh, they most assuredly would. However, as I do not hold Patents of Magic, they would have me jailed on sight, or worse," I explained.

"That seems silly," she mused. "If you're trying to stop a necromancer, I should think they would want to lend any assistance they could. Patents or not."

"In a perfect world, they would. But as I am not allowed to

practice magic within the borders of Eldemy, they'll assume I'm up to no good. And because I am without patents, it's unlikely they'd believe me if I were to explain why I violated my banishment," I said.

"It's still silly," she said.

"Well, yes and no," I said. "There are far more examples of un- or dis-patented mages who shouldn't be allowed to live, let alone practice magic. Some of them are very bad. Very dangerous. The Cardinal Mages' reasons are sound, and they do not make exceptions, unfortunately," I said.

"There's also the fact that we played some small part in the death of Basma, Cardinal Mage of the South. That would be considered a capital crime, punishable by hanging," I said.

I was now regretting this whole affair. Basma was a legend when I was studying at the Collegium. I remembered that several students wished to become Basma's apprentice. He was often called 'the most powerful battle mage in memory.' It was said that his power with the Force of fire was so great that he could bring down massive storms of fire upon a battlefield as if a volcano had erupted.

I'd heard rumors that his ability with the Force of earth was so great that he could bend and manipulate gravity itself. He would have been a powerful asset against Marwoleth, should the Duke and his Cardinal Mages get involved.

But I was also glad Basma didn't get a chance to bring his considerable power against the Scarab. If he had that opportunity, we would all be prisoners or more likely dead.

Kidal returned to the top of the forecastle to join us again. He brought with him two more filled cups. I looked down at my cup and realized I'd only taken one sip. I quickly finished it as he approached. It truly was a fine brown ale.

Kidal again handed me an ale-filled cup, and I raised it to him again. He mimicked the gesture.

71

"I informed the quartermaster that I will escort you once we get to Lovers' Isle. You might need protection. There may be more settlers there than when you were last there, I suspect," Kidal announced.

"I don't think that's necessary," I said. While the defenses of my cottage were good, I wished to keep its location secret.

"I insist," he said with finality.

"Look, Kidal. You do not owe me a debt for your life," I started.

"I know I don't. That was repaid. In full," he said.

"What?" I asked.

"Kidal jumped into the harbor and pulled you out after you fell in," Jass explained.

I turned to Kidal. "You did?"

He shrugged. It was only then, days after the incident with the Duchess Adina, that I realized my staff was missing. It must have fallen in the water or been shattered by the impact of the cannonball.

I thought to ask after it but decided against it. I could make another when I had time.

"Also, when you get to Eldemy, I should like to escort you," he said.

"What? What about the Scarab?" I said.

"I'm done with piracy," he said bitterly. "It's too dangerous. I pirate's life is a short one. And I wish to live long enough to spend my share of the prize."

"I can't pay you," I said. The truth was I didn't want an armed escort. A well-dressed man with an armed escort screams "target" to bandits. The only more enticing target than a well-dressed man was a well-dressed man with an armed escort, as he truly must have something worth protecting.

"I don't expect it. My share of the Duchess Adina's prize is ... significant. I've been aboard the Scarab for five years. I've served under three captains and two quartermasters. And I've served on three ships before her. My luck has to be running out," he mused.

"Where we're going won't be without danger, and there might be a lot of it," I warned.

He waved a hand dismissively. "I've been in more than a score ship battles. What you face can't be more dangerous than the muzzles of a dozen cannon," he boasted.

"You may be surprised," I said.

CHAPTER TEN

The side trip to Lovers' Isle passed without incident.

I had found the long-abandoned cottage on this island just after I fled Eldemy.

I was barely seventeen when I was expelled from the Collegium. They attempted to jail me, but I was able to evade capture. I spent two days in hiding, thanks to an innkeeper I'd made friends with. He kept me safe and booked passage aboard a ship bound for the Outer Isles.

During that time, my mind was filled with paranoid thoughts. I didn't know who to trust. While the crew of that ship seemed friendly, I suspected they might have recognized me.

When the ship stopped at Lovers' Isle to pick up more passengers and let a few off, I slipped off the ship and disappeared into the dense jungle.

I found the cottage purely by happenstance. I carried only a backpack with few supplies and a lot of superfluous items. I was nearly dying of thirst and decided that I might find a brook or a stream at the bottom of one of the many green valleys. I picked one and shambled onward.

That's when I found the cottage. My cottage. It was made of stone, with a wooden frame for a roof. The thatch roof had long since rotted away. And running next to the cottage was a stream of clear, cool water.

I spent the next few days attempting to repair the thatch roof, which I did, somewhat. I'm no thatcher, but the necessary materials were plentiful.

Once the cottage had a roof, I cleaned it out, intending to live there in hiding. There were probably two or three generations of dried and dead leaves within the stone cottage, and as I cleaned all the detritus out, I discovered two dried corpses, buried deep in the rotted leaves.

As best I could tell, they were a husband and wife, for the two corpses were entwined in an embrace when I came upon them.

I buried them behind the cottage. I wondered if they were the lovers that gave Lovers' Isle its name, but I realized no one named places for common folk. It was likely they just emigrated here, hoping for a better life. In a rotted purse, barely tied to the husband's belt, I found nine gold coins, twenty silver coins and nineteen copper coins. It was more money than I had seen in my entire life.

It was the kind of wealth that rivaled what my parents had worked for their entire lives.

Soon I yearned for human companionship: someone, anyone, I could talk to. Since I had spent so much time and effort making this place my home, I decided to hide it. I put up scry walls as best I could and an enchantment that would hide the cottage from casual passersby.

Even though it had been more than a decade since I'd been to the cottage, I knew the way here easily. I led the way as Jass and Kidal struggled to keep up.

We made our way from the small harbor on the south side of the island to the mountainous interior. Lovers' Isle was teeming with life, some of it dangerous. More than once, Kidal called my attention to a venomous snake or other crawling creature.

When we arrived at that familiar valley, I picked up my pace, curious about what I would find after more than a decade.

I found my small cottage, nestled in a thick, jungle-filled valley, in good order.

My head now felt better, so I attempted to call forth the Force of magic to dispel my enchantments.

Both Jass and Kidal gasped as the last of my enchantments unraveled, revealing to them for the first time my cottage.

"It's a stone hut," Kidal said.

"Cottage," I corrected.

"This was your home?" Kidal asked.

"Only for a while. Then I moved on to Ecota Isle. I haven't been back here since," I said.

We entered the place. It was a one-room cottage, containing a makeshift mattress I'd put together, but it had long rotted away. There was a fireplace and a few rusted pots and pans I'd scavenged from the previous owners. I hadn't left anything of value here, as I didn't know if I would ever return.

Kidal muscled the mirror through the narrow door, followed by Jass with the wooden chest. I directed them to set them in the middle of the floor.

I spent nearly two hours rebuilding my scry walls and wards, protecting the cottage from magical snooping and random passersby.

We made our way back to the Scarab and continued our journey to Eldemy.

As we made our way to a dock on the southern outskirts of the Great City of Eldemy, Jass asked me a question that must have been burning in her mind, and I was quite surprised it had taken her this long.

"How did you put up the shield that stopped the cannonball so quickly? You certainly didn't have time to mutter the rhymes for the Forces you used," she said.

"That's quite right," I said. "The various rhymes, the limericks, quatrains and sonnets, are only tools. They help put you in the correct mindset to summon and control the Forces, by visualizing the symbols of each Force," I explained.

She looked confused.

"Once you've mastered the rhymes of the Forces, you will over time become accustomed to how the words play within your mind. As this ..." I searched for the right term, "feeling becomes familiar, you will be able to attain it without the use of the rhymes. It takes a great deal of time and practice, but you'll get there. Of that, I have no doubt," I said.

"Is it dangerous to do that?" she asked.

"It can be. For example, I would never attempt that with the Force of earth. It is not my forte, and I always struggled with it. But with the Forces of air and bolstering, which I used for the shield, I know them quite well," I said.

While what I told her wasn't exactly untrue, I didn't explain that I had unleashed, rather than called in a controlled way, both of those Forces. The mass and velocity of the cannonball were quite substantial, and my shield was more of a desperation move, but I wasn't going to tell her that.

In fact, it is likely that the time it took me to heal was a result of the unleashing of those Forces. Much of the damage I received was likely of my own doing.

As we slowly tacked into the southern harbor, we could see the Great City of Eldemy in the distance.

It was a sprawl of stone and wood buildings, with the great white spires of the duke's palace dominating the scene, along with the towers of the citadels of the four Cardinal Mages, which were spread across the city.

The outer stone walls that defended the great city loomed over the homes and hovels of those who could not afford a place within in walls, not that it mattered. There hadn't been a war that threatened the city of Eldemy in more than three generations.

I looked down at the ring on my finger. The small pearl-like stone was now a dark gray. I frowned at it.

"When we get to the city, will we have time to see the sights?"

Jass asked.

"We're not going to the city," I said, looking back at my ring. "We're as close as we're going to get, I think."

Jass looked at me with disappointment.

"I'm sorry, Jass. It's just not safe for me there," I explained.

She shrugged, but she was still disappointed.

"When we get to the city, I will need to equip myself," Kidal announced from behind me.

Jass's eyebrows shot up in excitement.

"We're not going there," I said.

"We must. Or at least I must. This little blade won't do," he said, brandishing his dagger with a skilled flourish. "And I'll need armor. Now that I'm on dry land." He raised his eyebrows at me and grinned.

"We can find a blacksmith on the outskirts," I said.

"Nothing but the best will do, and that will be in the city proper. Besides, I can afford it now," he answered with another grin. I was beginning to realize what he was up to.

"I supposed we can wait here," I said reluctantly. "As long as you're not too long."

"Can I go with him?" Jass asked excitedly.

Kidal and I answered at the same time, except I said, "no," and Kidal said, "certainly." I rolled my eyes. I was not going to win this battle.

"I'll keep an eye on here. No one will dare accost her if I'm escorting her," Kidal said.

I looked up at the tall, large, dark-skinned man. He was probably right. He was more than a head taller than I, and far broader. His muscular chest and arms would certainly act as a deterrent.

I realized I'd never seen him in a shirt.

"Do you own any shirts, Kidal?" I asked.

"One. For special occasions. I'll pick up sōme in the city," he said looking at the Eldemy skyline.

"Very well, but please be back before nightfall. There's an inn nearby. It's called the Bonny Scarecrow. I'll arrange for rooms and dinner," I said resignedly.

"But please don't be too long," I pleaded.

"We won't!" Jass exclaimed. "Thank you Mandeight!" She gave me an enormous hug.

I reached for my purse and pulled out some of its contents and counted out ten silver coins.

"Here's some money," I said, handing it to Jass. "Buy yourself something to remember the visit, but don't pay the asking price. Haggle them down. Kidal can help you with that."

"Big spender!" Kidal said with a wink. "I'll make sure she isn't cheated."

They left, and I watched the big man and the slight, young girl walk away in the morning light toward Eldemy. Jass's red curls flounced as she hurried to keep up with Kidal's long strides.

I walked through Southtown, which is what the locals called the sprawl to the South of Eldemy.

I had spent much of my time when I was excused from the Collegium here in Southtown. Street vendors lined the narrow roads that wended their way through the sprawling landscape. Some displayed treasures brought in from ships, probably pirate vessels. Some offered culinary delights made from the sea creatures from the harbor.

The smell of Southtown hit me like a ton of bricks: the acrid smell of smoking fish, the perfume of women offering other wares, the stench of horse dung and worse.

I hired a boy to help with our belongings as I made my way to the Bonny Scarecrow. I handed him ten copper coins to hire a horse and wagon, telling him to keep what was left.

Though I had not been here in nearly two decades, I was able to find the Bonny Scarecrow without much problem. It had been my inn of choice prior to my banishment.

The sign over the inn was, in fact, a miniature scarecrow. The sight of it made me shudder slightly. Scarecrows were nothing to trifle with, even small ones.

I entered the inn and paid the boy when he finished carrying our things in.

"Basil, I'll need three rooms – third floor, if they're available. And be so kind as to draw me a bath," I said without looking up. I had said that phrase in this place many times in the distant past, though the number of rooms had changed, of course.

"Mandeight?" I heard a disturbingly old voice answer.

I looked up to see Basil Turnwell, the owner and proprietor of the Bonny Scarecrow. The last twenty years had not been kind to him. He was still tall and gaunt, but his height was now betrayed by a curved spine that made him seem much shorter. His mane of black hair had turned sparse and gray. He still wore the livery from his days in the duke's household staff.

He had been the duke's head butler, and he used his savings upon his retirement to purchase the Scarecrow. As a result, his establishment was known for the best service outside of the Duke's palace, and some say it even rivaled that.

He walked around the desk and stood before me. A faint smile washed over his face, starting first with his eyes and moving to his mouth.

"It is a pleasure to see you again, Master Mandeight. I must say that I am very glad to see you well," he said with the formality only a butler could manage. Then he looked around, "but where are your traveling companions?"

"They're off in the city," I answered. "They insisted on shopping."

"Do you still offer maid and valet services?" I asked. The Scarecrow was one of the few establishments where commoners could experience how the high-born lived.

"We do indeed, Master Mandeight," he answered excitedly.

"Excellent. I should like to hire a valet and maid for my traveling companions, Master Kidal and Young Mistress Jass," I said. It would be a nice treat for them, I thought. Once we set out to find our dark mage, we would know very little comfort.

"Very good, Master Mandeight. I shall assign Isabelle to the young mistress and Jasper to Master Kidal," he said. He reached out and tapped a bell on his desk, and no sooner had the ring faded, a young footman emerged from a doorway behind the desk.

"Take Master Mandeight's things to rooms 31, 33 and 35, and have Maddie prepare a bath for the good master," Basil said.

"Yes, Mister Turnwell," the footman said.

I indicated which items belonged in which rooms and turned back to Basil.

"What's on the menu, Basil?" I asked.

"The cook has prepared duck with a lemon glaze, a venison pudding and of course our beef stew, as always," he announced.

"Just the beef stew, Basil. I'm afraid I'm too hungry to enjoy something dear. Oh, and a pitcher of ale" I said.

Basil winced. "Do you not wish to hear the wine list?" he asked cautiously.

I smiled. "I'm sorry Basil. I've been aboard ship for more than a fortnight. I'm afraid I've grown accustomed to ale," I replied.

"Well, are you sure you wouldn't want a more opulent meal? Sailors' cooking can often dull the senses," he offered, as he walked me to a table in the corner.

"You know, the cook aboard the ship was actually rather talented," I began. "Apparently they stole him ...." I stopped, as I was about to tell him that the pirate vessel I was on stole the cook from one of the Duke's ships. "... from a very nice restaurant on one of the outer isles," I amended.

He made a pained expression.

"Alright, Basil, bring me the duck. But I warn you I may order the stew as well. I'm terribly hungry," I said.

"I'll see if the cook can manage a double portion," he said with a satisfied smile.

After the meal, which was very good, I'd finished most of the pitcher of ale and was ready for my bath, which was wonderful.

It was now getting rather late, and Jass and Kidal had not yet returned. Though I tried not to, I began to worry. I dressed quickly and made my way downstairs.

I walked up to the desk, where Basil dutifully stood.

"How was your bath, Master Mandeight?" he asked.

"Wonderful. I think I managed to get most of the sea salt off," I said, and he replied with a polite chuckle.

Then I leaned forward and whispered, "can I speak privately to you, Basil?"

"Of course," he said, matching my tone. He rang the bell and instructed the footman to watch the desk.

I followed Basil into the back room. He closed the door behind us.

"What can I do for you, Mandeight?" he asked. His air of butler formality was gone in an instant. Basil played the part of a butler well, but he was also a friend and one who knew my past. In fact, he had proved to be a good and true friend, and they are rare.

"I'm getting worried about my fellow travelers. They should have been here by now," I said quickly.

He looked out of his office window and said, "it is starting to turn dark. You think they may have been waylaid?"

"I doubt it," I said. I couldn't see any young tough being stupid enough to attempt to waylay Kidal. "But Kidal has been at sea for some time. I could see him ... blowing off too much steam."

"They don't put up with that sort of thing in the city," he mused.

"Do you still have contacts with the guard?" I asked.

"Of course," he said, looking through his desk. He set out a parchment and quill. "Write down their descriptions and I'll fetch a boy to check with the jailer. I'll be back in a moment."

I wrote out the descriptions of both Kidal and Jass and handed it to Basil upon his return with a teen-aged boy. He handed it to the boy and whispered instructions.

It was near midnight when the boy returned. I had camped out at a table in the dining room, and Basil made sure I had plenty of hot coffee to blunt the effects of the pitcher of ale. The boy hurried into the back office and left a moment later. Basil appeared in the doorway and motioned with his head for me to join him.

"Any luck?" I asked, walking in his backroom.

"Yes. But it's not good news," he sighed. "They are both jailed. It seems this Kidal struck a guardsman, a sergeant, in fact."

I bowed my head in defeat.

"Don't despair, Mandeight. We can get them out, but I'm afraid it will cost you," Basil said.

"How much?" I asked with a frown.

"That'll be up to the jailer. He's a friend, but the sergeant your companion struck will raise a stink, I'm afraid. Take what you have with you. I can reopen your account if that's not enough," Basil offered.

"That's kind of you, Basil. I'll collect my things and go," I said as I headed for the door.

"Uh, Mandeight," he interrupted.

"Yes?"

"You took a great risk coming back here, as I'm sure you're aware," he started. "And the boy spotted Xavier around the jail. You don't think he knows you're here, do you?"

I looked down at my ring. It was the same shade of dark gray, but I knew it would soon be black.

"I can't see how, unless they talked," I said.

"Is that a possibility?" he asked.

"No," I started. Jass certainly knew of my situation, but then I realized Kidal did not. I closed my eyes. "Oh gods. Kidal might have. He might have name-dropped to spare himself jail time." I let out a groan of consternation.

"Would you like me to come with?" he offered.

"You won't talk Xavier out of jailing me," I said.

"He might relent, perhaps. Given your relationship," he said.

I laughed. "You didn't have any siblings, did you, Basil?"

"No. I'm afraid not. But certainly, your reason for returning is good, at least I assume it's good," he said.

"It is," I confirmed.

"Perhaps if you explain…" Basil said as I cut him off.

"No. He won't believe me," I said.

I looked at Basil's long, gaunt face, as a devilish expression, one that contrasted with his age, crossed his face.

"Then perhaps I could create a distraction," he said with a sly smile.

"The last time was a very close call. Are you sure you want to risk that?" I said, looking at him carefully. "Neither of us are as young as we used to be."

Basil had been referring to my last escape, nearly twenty years earlier, when he had distracted Xavier long enough for me to secretly exit the Bonny Scarecrow and sneak aboard an outbound ship.

"He never figured it out the last time. I think it should be safe to try again," Basil said.

"If you say so," I said hesitantly.

"I'll go change into something more larcenous whilst you prepare," he said, as he made his way to the stairs in the lobby.

Two hours later, well past midnight, I walked downstairs into the lobby.

Basil was dressed in a simple white shirt, black breeches and a black woolen overcoat. We nodded to each other and I followed him out the back entrance into the alley.

I handed Basil a pack.

"Be careful with that. They're loaded," I joked. The pack was filled with small enchanted jars. Each contained kerosene along with various metal shavings and each jar held a fire enchantment. Fire wasn't my forte, but I had taken pains to make sure the enchantments were sound.

"I remember. I'll go a few blocks away and throw them about," Basil said.

"And don't let Xavier find you," I warned. "If he sees you he might put two and two together. Maths aren't his forte, but he's not a dolt. This is the exact same distraction we used when I fled Eldemy."

"I shall disappear into the mists," he said with feigned mystery.

I smiled at him, and he returned it with a wolfish grin, which was far more youthful than it should have been.

"You know, Basil, you might have made a formidable bandit in your day," I teased as we walked.

"I much preferred being a formidable head butler," he said with dignity.

CHAPTER ELEVEN

I stood in the shadows of an alley across from the city jails, and just as I feared, the jailer stood at the entrance speaking with Xavier.

Xavier was the stereotypical mage: tall and thin, with a long white beard and even longer mane of white hair. I wondered if he dyed his hair white. I'd hardly grayed at all, and he was only a decade or so my senior. He was dressed in the pale blue robes of his station as Cardinal Mage of the West.

Twice Xavier looked toward the alley, and each time I tried to think invisible thoughts. No, mages can't turn invisible, though right at that moment, I wished I could.

The jailer, who was Basil's contact, mimicked his interest in the alley each time. The jailer was short and pudgy. He was dressed in the same livery as the town guard: the gray and gold tunic with a dragon's head emblazoned upon the chest. But the livery was but a parody of the grandeur it should have conveyed, as it fit the man very poorly. It was too tight at some points and too loose in others. Clearly, the jailer's job didn't require much exertion, not that I was in any condition to comment on his portliness. He had a wooden cudgel tucked in his belt and on the opposite side was a giant ring of iron keys.

Gasmer, Basil had given me the jailer's name, had a mop of dark brown hair that hadn't been attended to in weeks or months. His face was ruddy with recent exertion, probably from running out to meet and glad-hand Xavier.

The Eldemy city jails were built with the same stone as the other government buildings in the city. The structure was white, though, in the gloomy shadows of night and the sparse lantern light, it looked more gray and yellow than white. It a was single-story structure with twelve large columns standing at the front, but I knew there were two basement – or dungeon – levels below this pretty stone facade.

When Xavier looked toward me a third time, I knew he was sensing something. He began to walk toward the alley, and the jailer's face turned nervous and even redder.

Just then, Basil pulled my ass out of the fire as he began setting off my makeshift fireworks show. Great explosions and flashes of bright orange light filled the sky from several blocks away, near the center of the city.

Xavier stopped, looked at the light show and barked something to the jailer. Then he headed off the other direction, not quite running, but walking very quickly, his robes billowing as he left.

The jailer looked around and motioned for me to approach.

"I could see you myself there, what with all the moving and peaking about!" Jailer Gasmer hissed.

"Sorry. I needed a good vantage point," I said.

"Come, come. We don't have much time," he said extending his palm greedily.

I handed him a small leather pouch, and he quickly emptied the contents into his palm. He frowned and looked at me with a sidelong glare.

I gave him an impatient motion with my head. He looked down at the coin, not an insignificant amount, and looked me in the eye again.

"Our friend said he would be good for the balance," I whispered.

He eyed me suspiciously, then said, "alright. Go back to your hiding place, but stay still, damn you!"

"Yeah, yeah," I muttered as I walked back to the shadows.

A few minutes later, Kidal emerged from the jail with a full-size steel corslet hanging from one arm and a long maille shirt draped over his shoulder. Jass followed right behind, dressed in a pink and white dress, complete with a crinoline underskirt if I was not mistaken. I rolled my eyes.

The jailer then emerged and pointed to the alley where I was hidden. They both ran toward me. Jass looked both terrified and relieved, almost to the point of tears.

Kidal's greeted me with a wide smile, and he was barely able to contain his laughter. I didn't know if his cheery mood was the result of his escape or a natural revelry.

I escorted them to a side gate that Basil explained would be left open for us, and we made our way to the Bonny Scarecrow.

It was nearly dawn when we entered the Scarecrow. Basil was sitting alone in the dining room with a bottle of wine and a cup. His head and shoulders drooped in relief when we entered.

"All went well on your end, I suppose," he said.

"It did. Thank you, Basil. I'm afraid our friend wanted more than I had, but Kidal will be happy to make up the difference once you know what it is," I said.

"What?' Kidal asked.

"Never you mind," I snapped. "I emptied my purse on account of you, and this gaffer risked life and limb as well!"

"Gaffer!?" Basil exclaimed. "Might I remind you I made it back here before you lot. 'Gaffer' indeed!"

"Alright. Point taken," I laughed. "Pour me some of that, will you?" I nodded to the bottle.

"I thought you were an ale man now," Basil said wryly. I waved is comment away with a hand as I approached the table. Basil was drenched with sweat, as was his shirt. He'd removed the black woolen jacket he had donned when we left.

I dropped myself into a chair. "Basil Turnwell, this is Kidal and

Jass, my apprentice," I said for introductions.

"I wouldn't mind some of that," Kidal said, dropping his corslet and maille on the floor. He was breathing heavily from the run from the city as he sat down.

"Can I have some?" Jass asked.

"No," the three of us said simultaneously.

Basil pushed me the newly filled cup and handed Kidal the bottle.

"Much obliged," Kidal said, lifting the bottle for a long pull.

I raised the cup to Basil and drank. He was now sitting with a much straighter back. And he somehow looked a bit younger.

"You need to get out more," I told him. "The exercise has done you well."

"Nothing gets the blood moving like a good jailbreak," he said, rising to fetch another glass. "Don't kill that bottle, Kidal, or I'll make you pay for it."

I looked at Jass. She was forlorn and sad.

"That's a lovely dress, Jass. Very ladylike," I said. She looked up, but her expression didn't change.

"Basil, could you pour a cup of small beer for the young mistress and perhaps bring a pitcher of your brown. It's quite nice," I said. "Come, Jass, sit down."

"Just a moment!" Basil bellowed.

He walked over and pulled out a chair and said very formally, "young mistress." He nodded to the chair. She sat down as he adjusted the chair for her. Her expression turned to a blushing smile.

When Basil returned from the kitchen, he brought with him a tray with four cups and a pitcher. He set it all out, poured the ale and joined us.

"Who'd you knock?" he asked, not looking up. Basil was speaking of the sergeant guard Kidal had punched.

"Didn't get his name, but he was an ass," Kidal said.

"What did he look like?" Basil asked.

"Red hair. Redder face," Kidal answered.

"Bertrand. He is an ass," Basil said. Kidal laughed.

"I hope we didn't put you out, Master Basil," Kidal said.

"Oh, not at all. Especially if you're paying the short of the bill to the jailer," Basil said with a sly smile.

"About that," I said to Basil. He smiled back. "The jailer took all I had, I'm afraid."

"I'll pay the inn bill," Kidal said.

"Oh good. I was hoping not to reopen Master Mandeight's line of credit," Basil said. "You still want the valet and maid, Mandeight?"

"What?" Kidal said.

"Of course! They need a treat after their ordeal," I said before Kidal could object. He answered with a whimpering moan.

I looked over at Jass and noticed something different. It was her hair. Her red locks had a natural but subtle curl to them, but now her hair fell in ringlets and reacted to every movement of her head.

"Jass. Did you get your hair done?" I asked.

"I did!" she said with a bright smile. She turned her head back and forth, and the curls bounced and flounced with every movement.

It was also obvious that she was ... more developed than I had previously noted. The dress seemed to accentuate the young woman's curves; and the upper part of her dress, built more like a bodice, accentuated that portion of her body as well. I decided not to comment on all that.

"You are a lovely sight, indeed, young mistress," Basil added. Jass beamed.

"I should say," I began, "Basil, here, is an old and dear friend. He purchased this place when he retired as head butler to the Duke."

Both Kidal's and Jass's eyes went wide.

"Should I have curtsied?" Jass asked. Kidal and I both laughed.

Basil shut us down with a frown and clearing of his throat.

"One only curtsies for the high-born nobility, young mistress. As a butler, I was but a member of the household staff, though it's head. For one of my station, you need only stand when I stand or enter the room. But that was only when I was a butler. Now, I'm just a humble innkeep. But it's good of you to ask these questions. Many young people think nothing of propriety," he said.

She nodded to him, smiling.

"Finish your beer and head off to bed, Jass. While we won't get the early start I had hoped for, I do want to leave sometime tomorrow morning," I said. She gulped down the small beer and began to stand.

"Wait!" Basil said.

He stood and held her chair as she rose. She unsuccessfully stifled a small smile and laugh as she began to walk away.

"I'll show you to your room, young mistress. Let me know when you wish to be awakened, and I'll have your maid draw you a bath and then dress you," Basil said as they walked away.

After I knew they were out of earshot, I turned to Kidal.

"What possessed you to strike a sergeant guard?" I asked. "Not to mention that you got Jass jailed as well!"

"Oh, she did that on her own. That guard said something rude to her, and she punched him. I'm just the one who knocked him out," Kidal said defensively.

"What did the guard say?" I asked.

"I don't know, and Jass wouldn't say. She just said it was very rude," Kidal said.

"Good for her, I suppose," I said.

Kidal and I finished the ale, and Basil soon joined us and finished the bottle of wine.

CHAPTER TWELVE

I woke up around midday, much later than I intended, and I was still groggy. I was gladdened to discover that my headache had gone completely.

I had arranged with Basil to store Jass's new dress, as she would have no opportunity to wear it where we were going. He also sent one of his staff out to procure her proper traveling clothes. He offered to put it on Kidal's tab, but I asked him to reopen my line of credit, which he did.

When I came down to the dining room, Kidal and Jass were already down there. Jass was wearing her new traveling clothes, which, although not as fancy as her dress, were quite smart.

She wore typical working-class traveling attire: light gray cotton breeches with a long-sleeve matching jacket with a simple white shirt beneath. Including with her traveling clothes was a cotton backpack, which she had dutifully packed and was now on the ground, leaning against her chair.

"Mandeight!" she said. "Come join us!"

I did, of course.

"Don't eat so much, Jass," Kidal pleaded.

"Now, now. She's still a growing girl, and you put her through quite an ordeal," I chided with a smile.

Kidal frowned, but a small smile crossed his face. No doubt he knew he was now paying penance for last evening's escapades.

"How much did that corslet set you back?" I asked of him.

"I don't want to talk about it," Kidal said as he shoveled food into his maw while guarding it with an arm wrapped around his plate.

"Excuse me, please," Jass said as she motioned to Basil. He hurried over and held her chair as she rose.

I looked in the corner, and Kidal's corslet and maille were hanging on tee stands. The corslet gleamed with a mirror finish, and they must have sanded his maille shirt, for it shined as well.

"Look, Kidal! Your valet polished your armor," I exclaimed.

"Yeah, I saw," he said glumly. "I would much rather have had the maid. Did you get a look at her?" he said in a conspiratorial voice.

"No, I haven't, but they don't offer those sorts of services here," I said.

Then I whispered, "We can go to one of those establishments when we don't have the girl with us. I know of a good place. Very clean, and the women are beautiful. But you'll pay."

Kidal gave me a devilish grinned.

"Jass has been going on about her lady's maid, you know. Talked about it all morning. Do you think that's wise?" Kidal asked.

"I don't think there's any harm in a treat now and then," I said.

"But what if she thinks this whole trip is going to be like this? I have a strong suspicion it won't," he said flatly.

"No, it won't," I said. "I'll set her mind right soon enough, but for now, let her enjoy it. Besides, Basil enjoys pampering those who never get to be pampered, and Jass has had a hard life. She's an orphan, you know."

"I figured as much. Not many parents worth their salt would send their young daughters off with the likes of you," he said, eyeing me over his plate.

"It's not like that," I protested.

"I know," he said with a placating gesture. "But you have the look of a man who gets in trouble. And that doesn't even account for the fact that you're a mage. Mages get in a lot of trouble."

"That's true enough," I admitted. "I've been thinking the same thing myself. I was thinking of leaving her here. Basil does love to dote on those who have been deprived."

"You think she would stand for it? No, wait! I don't even know what we're doing. Why did you come here? I got the impression you're not supposed to be here," Kidal said.

"I'm not," I admitted. "I'm not a patented mage, and as such, I was banished from the Duchy of Eldemy."

"Then why risk returning," he asked.

"There's a dark mage. He set traps on Ecota Isle. That's how I met Jass. Whoever he is, he took her mother many years ago," I said.

"Why not tell the authorities and go about your life?" he asked.

"It's not that simple. They won't believe me. Without patents, I have no credibility. Most mages without patents turn to crime, or worse," I explained.

"So, you must handle it yourself," Kidal concluded.

"Just so," I said. "But it's likely to get dangerous. No place for her."

"Then it's settled," Kidal said.

"Well, yes and no," I began. I was conflicted. "She's at a dangerous point in her training. She knows enough to summon the Forces, but not enough to control them. Leaving her unsupervised is irresponsible."

"You don't have a friendly mage you could leave her with?" he asked.

"No. I have few friends in Eldemy, and none of them are mages," I said.

"Can Basil watch her?" Kidal asked.

"No. I can't expect that of him," I said. "I'm afraid we may have to take her with us. I don't see any other choice."

"But you just said we should leave her," Kidal said.

"I'm thinking out loud. Bad habit, I know," I replied. Kidal had spent most of his adult life under the command of captains and quartermasters. He was used to receiving and following orders. He clearly wasn't used to hearing commanders vacillate over what to do.

We sat in silence as Jass returned. This time Basil gestured to one of his footmen to hold her chair for her. He was young and handsome, and Jass smiled at him as she sat down, and to my consternation, the young footman smiled back. He looked to be only a few years older than Jass, and my reaction surprised me.

Was I becoming protective of Jass? Perhaps I was. At her age, parents were both protective and looking for proper suitors. Jass had no parents. Was I taking up that role? It is said that nature abhors a vacuum. Perhaps her lack of parents had wakened some parental instincts of my own. I found that prospect both ominous and annoying.

Training an apprentice was a lot of work and defending a girl's honor against flocks of post-pubescent boys sounded like even more work. Would she expect me to consult with her on possible suitors? Would she seek my blessing on such matters? I shuddered at the thought. Keeping her from blowing herself up was enough to keep my mind occupied, and I didn't need any of that other stuff muddying my thinking.

I put all that aside and decided to set her straight on our traveling conditions to find Marwoleth.
"Jass," I started, "we're going to be traveling across untamed country. No inns, no maids, no handsome footmen."

"I figured that," she said blushing slightly. I noted that she was stealing glances at the handsome young footman. I cleared my throat.

"I just want to make sure you know we won't be traveling in comfort. We'll be eating hard bread and cheese mostly. We might kill some game along the way, but it won't be easy," I added.

"Yes, I understand," she said, eyeing the footman, who was now standing in the corner at attention, occasionally stealing a glance toward her. I cleared my throat again, but much louder this time.

"If we find Marwoleth, we might not survive the confrontation," I said.

"Wait," Kidal interrupted. "Did you say Marwoleth?"

"Yes. That's the mage we're hunting," I said.

"Gods be kind," Kidal muttered with a gesture I had never seen before. It must have been a gesture of the religion of the Southerners. "I met him once. Many years ago."

Jass and I looked at each other in shock.

"You did," I said with great interest.

"Yes. I was just a loader then, with the Merry Finch, before she sank," Kidal said.

"What do you know of him?" I asked leaning forward with intense interest.

"He was aboard the Duke's Pride. She was the ship that sank us. I spent time in her brig. They said he was a mage from the shores to the West. From the Empire of the Sun," he said.

"'The Empire of the Sun?'" I asked. "I've never heard of it."

"Neither had I, nor any of us," Kidal admitted. "Never heard the term before or since. But he kept an undead as a retainer. The crew was terrified of him and his dead servant."

"They let him on the Duke's Pride with an undead?" I asked with disbelief.

"No, you misunderstand," Kidal said. "The Duke's Pride had been taken by pirates. She was a galleon the size of which you couldn't imagine. Eighty-two guns. Three rows of cannon on each side. The crew boasted that they'd made it to the Empire of the Sun. They said she was the only ship big enough to make such a trip. You would need a year or more of supplies, not to mention the storms that plague the seas beyond the far islands.

"It was almost as if Marwoleth ran the ship, but he was only a passenger on their return voyage," Kidal said. "I've never seen a crew with so much fear, even when they're about to die."

"And they were right," whispered Jass. "He's an old mage. A thousand years old or more." She gave me a significant look.

"Mages can live a thousand years?" Kidal said looking at us both with wonder and fear.

"No, not most of us. Most mages live no longer than anyone else," I corrected. "But some turn to a darker path, to darker powers that can extend their lives."

"But he looked to be a young man. No more than twenty or so," Kidal said.

"Perhaps he made himself younger," Jass suggested.

"Or he took a younger body," I added darkly.

"That's possible?" Kidal said with wide-eyed fear.

"It may be. This Marwoleth, if he is in fact the same mage we're tracking, has abilities with at least two Forces I have never encountered," I said.

"But you're not a real mage," Kidal said almost pleading. "Jass said you were kicked out, and you yourself admitted you have no patents. Maybe those are in advanced magic school."

I frowned at Jass. She shrugged apologetically.

"I assure you I know of all Forces taught at the Collegium. Even Jass has studied a text of all the Forces known there," I said.

"Maybe the teachers hide things from the students," Kidal suggested.

"That is possible. We certainly heard rumors of other more powerful and dangerous Forces, and those rumors may be based in fact," I admitted.

"How do you know he's so old?" Kidal asked.

"We found historical records on Ecota Isle confirming he's at least one hundred and seventy years old. And Mandeight had notes from historical records from Eldemy mentioning him thousands of years ago. He raised an undead army to lay siege to this city. And he was never captured," Jass added.

"I've seen no mention of the Empire of the Sun in the records of the Old Empire here. Perhaps he learned that magic across the Western Sea," I suggested. "Do you remember what he looked like?"

"He was short and slight. Dark, though not as dark as I. I only saw him once," Kidal said. "He was selecting prisoners from the brig of the Duke's Pride. They said something about a spell he was casting, and it terrified the crew."

"Did you ever find out what that spell was?" I asked.

"Only later," he said ominously.

"How did you escape?" I asked.

"The ship ran aground on the backside of Ecota Isle. It was a terrible storm. The ship split in two. I almost drown. There was no distinction between the crew and the prisoners then. We were all terrified trying not to drown in the boiling waters there. That's where I got most of my scars when I washed up to the reef. I barely lived," Kidal said.

"And what happened to Marwoleth?" Jass asked.

"I don't know. About ten of us made it to shore. A few prisoners and a few crew. We helped each other get on land. The mage wasn't there," Kidal answered. "That's when we discovered his spell."

"How so?" I asked.

"We'd only been ashore a short time, and they started walking out of the water," he said staring blankly at his food. It was clear his appetite was gone.

"Who walked out of the water?" I asked.

"The undead. Dozens of them. I recognized some as the prisoners the mage selected. Some were from a cell next to mine. Their part of the ship sunk and they drowned. But he brought them all back," Kidal said.

Jass looked at me with a searching expression, as if she were trying to read my thoughts. I realized it wouldn't be hard. If my face showed half the fear I felt, I would have looked bloody terrified.

Finally, Jass asked, "What's wrong?"

"I know nothing of necromancy, of course, but I do know the kind of concentration magic requires. I know the kind of powerful Forces you must muster to cast such magic at a distance. Not to mention the fact that he was on a sinking ship in a massive storm." I said.

"I don't think I could pull off anything like that, with any Force, and if he survived it..." I started.

"He's way more powerful than you," Kidal said completing my sentence.

"By several orders of magnitude," I said.

Kidal and I exchanged a significant glance, then I looked to Jass, and she was almost scowling at me.

"What was the size of the crew?" I asked, changing the subject.

"I can't say. Two hundred, maybe more. I know we received a full barrage from the Duke's Pride. Forty-one guns. That's at least eighty-two men crewing the cannons, just on the starboard side. They may have had crew for larboard as well. That's one hundred sixty just on cannon. There must have been three dozen above. She had nine masts," Kidal said.

"Nine masts?" I exclaimed. "I've never heard of a ship so large. Are you sure?"

"Yes. It was sunset when they reached us. I got a good look at her silhouette. We were in doldrums when they caught us. Their sails billowed like there was a gale. We assumed they had a mage on board then," Kidal said.

"No doubt," I added. "I hate to say it, but this may be beyond us."

Just then Basil approached our table.

"Would it seem too familiar to the good masters and young mistress if I were to join you?" he asked with his make-believe formality.

"Sit, Basil," I said plainly not wanting to engage in feigned nobility.

His face grew serious and he sat.

"Why do you all look so morose?" Basil asked.

"We're discussing our mission, and that fact that we'll all die," Kidal said plainly.

"It's really that bad?" Basil asked.

"It is," Jass answered. "We're after a very powerful mage thousands of years old."

Basil leaned back in his chair in shock.

"I didn't know such a thing was possible," he said.

"It is, apparently," I answered.

"Mandeight, I am loath to bring it up, but you might want to reach out to Xavier. He is your brother, after all," he said.

I winced. I silently cursed Basil and his mouth.

Jass looked at me.

"Wait. Xavier Birdstaff, the Cardinal Mage of the West, is your brother?" she said in wonder.

"We don't get along," I explained quickly, trying to change the subject.

"So your family name is Birdstaff? Like a bird's pizzle?" Kidal asked, a small grin cracking through his downtrodden expression.

"It's an unfortunate name," I admitted.

Kidal tried, quite unsuccessfully, to stifle a laugh.

"Why don't you get along?" Jass asked ignoring Kidal's laughter.

"He's the one who turned me in for experimenting with magic. That's why I was expelled from the Collegium," I answered.

"Your own brother turned you in?" Kidal asked. "He must be an enormous ass. Or you are."

I looked at Basil. He shrugged apologetically.

"Yes, thank you. He's the most obstinate rules follower I've ever known," I said. "And it was a minor infraction at most. No one was killed or hurt. No cities plunged to the earth. It was a very minor fire, and I put it out myself very quickly."

Jass looked at me with surprise.

"I never said I didn't experiment. In fact, I said I did," I said in my own defense.

"Would he help us?" Kidal asked.

"No. I do not think he would," I answered.

"Perhaps I could approach him. He no doubt remembers me from my time with the Duke," Basil offered.

"This is a bad idea," I announced.

"You said this task was beyond us," Kidal said. "Is it beyond us if we have this Xavier with us?"

"Possibly," I answered. "A mage who has been plying the art for nearly three thousand years will have power and skills that would rival any assemblage of mages I can imagine."

"Should we just leave it be then?" Kidal asked.

There was silence for a few very long moments. Jass was the first to speak.

"I won't leave it be," she said finally. "Marwoleth took my mother, and he must come to justice."

"There may not be enough mages in all of Eldemy to best him," I said.

"I don't care. We can't, or at least I can't, sit by while someone takes people away from their families for whatever foul reason. What if he's planning another siege of Eldemy?" Jass pressed.

"Then he's going to succeed," I said.

"Do you want to live in that world, Mandeight? Do any of you?" she asked of the table.

There was silence.

"I certainly don't," she answered.

"You're not supposed to answer your own rhetorical questions," I said.

"Shut up, Mandeight. This is serious. Stop with the witty jokes," she said, raising her voice.

What will you do if this Marwoleth wins the day? What if he turns Eldemy into some awful undead empire? You think he's going to stop there?" she asked.

I felt as if I'd been smacked in the face. I often lost sight of the fact that Jass had lost her only family to this mage.

"I can hide pretty well," Kidal said.

"Oh really? What are you going to do if he turns his eye to the South? What if he brings your homeland into his undead rule? Or whatever he's got planned? Or this Empire of the Sun? What if it's already fallen? What's the use of surviving if you're left in a nightmare of a world?" Jass said. "I won't have it. If I have to die trying to stop him, that's better than living under his boot."

"Well said, young mistress," Basil said.

Basil sat up straight. Kidal and I slumped.

"I hold writs as a Friend of the Duke," Basil announced with sudden realization. "I can invite Xavier here as such. There are certain protocols he would have to follow, as I know he holds such writs himself, as do the other Cardinal Mages. We cannot simply give up and hide hoping things will just turn out alright.

"I owe it to His Grace to at least try. You three are not subjects of the Duke, I assume, but I am, and with that comes certain responsibilities. If you leave me what proof you have of this Marwoleth, I will present it myself, if need be," Basil said.

"We just got away from Xavier's clutches not eight hours ago, and now you want to invite him here?" I exclaimed.

"He won't know I was involved in that," Basil said.

"Xavier won't believe you if he knows it came from me," I said.

"Never you mind that. I must try. For the good of the duchy, I must try," Basil said.

"I will present it with you, Master Basil," Jass said.

"As will I," said Kidal with a bit of reluctance.

The three of them looked at me.

"Damn it!" I said.

This was the last thing I wanted. I wasn't even supposed to be here, and if Xavier wished, he could report me to the Masters of the Collegium. Those old and powerful mages could find me with little difficulty and imprison me. The last thing I wanted to do was languish in a stinking, rotting cell.

Then again, at least four of the most powerful mages in the duchy, well three actually, would know of Marwoleth. Perhaps they could do something about it. Hell, they might get the Masters of the Collegium involved. With them, they might be able to take him out. Imprisonment would be a small price to pay to avoid that kind of catastrophe.

I couldn't help to think that Jass's predictions were probably quite accurate. If Marwoleth, who had already attempted to take Eldemy once, tried it again, but with nearly three thousand more years of experience, he'd likely succeed.

And that truly would be a catastrophe. I'd studied Eldemic history extensively, and there had never been, at least in my reading, such a scenario.

Certainly, there had been powerful mages who had held perhaps far too much sway in the ducal courts of old. Some may have even been de facto leaders of the duchy for a time, though there was no written record of such mages. But that wasn't surprising. If a very powerful mage could hold sway over a ducal court, they would certainly be powerful enough to ensure their name never appeared in historical records unless they wished it to.

I recalled that both the siege of Eldemy by Marwoleth and the conventions that resulted in the Patents of Magic happened within the Eighth Millennia of the Sovereign Duchy of Eldemy, but they were separated by centuries. The siege happened in 7116, and the Conventions of Magic happened three hundred years later.

In fact, there had been no recorded incident regarding magic that seemed to be the impetus for the conventions. They just sort of happened. It was very likely whatever event led to the conventions never made it into historical records.

I sat in silence as Kidal, Jass and Basil stared at me intently. I let them stare.

What if Marwoleth's siege had been a distraction? If Marwoleth was adept with mind magic, he may have used the siege as a way to draw the Duke's forces to the walls, leaving the palace all but unguarded. He could have enslaved the Duke's mind, and the minds of his viziers, and become the power behind the throne without anyone knowing it.

Hell, he might have established the Patents of Magic to ensure that no other mage could ever match his power, and his dominance would last until he was tired of living.

But that didn't fit with the current facts. Why would Marwoleth have visited Ecota Isle not once but twice more than two thousand years later? Why would he have left a written record? Hubris? I could see a three-thousand-year-old mage being rather confident in their abilities.

Was he still the power behind the throne? Were Xavier and the other Cardinal Mages already enslaved by him? I found that hard to believe. Xavier was no slouch when it came to mind magic.

That's how he'd discovered my experimentation when we were at the Collegium.

My mind was getting away from me. It was as if Marwoleth was in my head, though I was reasonably sure he wasn't. Perhaps Marwoleth was legitimately bested on the field of battle and went into hiding. That better fit the facts at hand.

If he had somehow become immortal, he would have patience beyond comprehension. Perhaps he spent the last three millennia growing in power, preparing to try again.

What would happen to a mind that existed for three thousand years? Would he be capable of feeling sympathy or empathy for mere mortals? Did the endless string of years drive him mad? Is it possible that somewhere along the line, he ceased being a man and became a monster?

Jass' apocalyptic prediction might be rather optimistic. A world run by Marwoleth might be more of a night terror than a nightmare.

"Alright. Summon my hidebound twit of a brother," I relented. "I suppose a death from within the Eldemy jail would be quicker than hiding on an island. We have to at least try to stop this madman. If we don't, who will?"

CHAPTER THIRTEEN

Basil closed the Bonny Scarecrow the next day. We were washed, clothed and fed by the time Xavier Birdstaff, Cardinal Mage of the West, arrived.

I looked down at my ring, and the circular stone was now a dark black.

Much to my surprise, my estranged brother was accompanied by Samana, Cardinal Mage of the East.

Samana was about average height. She was young for a Cardinal Mage: no older than I. In fact, she had been one of my classmates. Her hair was curly and black. She had dark skin, though lighter than Kidal. I knew her family migrated from far south of High Fall, possibly from near Kidal's home. She wore robes of white and gray, indicating her station.

When she saw me, she began summoning defensive wards.

I rolled my eyes.

"Cardinal Mage! I am a Friend of the Duke, and I have summoned Xavier here as such. If you attend as well, you are under the same constraints. We meet for the good of the Sovereign Duchy, or we do not meet!" Basil exclaimed with far more force than I thought he could muster.

I wondered if this is how he spoke to his underlings when he was head butler of the Duke's palace.

He faced Samana, who was a formidable mage, without fear. I knew she was formidable, as she was one of the most talented mages in our class, perhaps the most talented. At the Collegium, I found her extremely intelligent and driven. I was not surprised she had attained the rank of Cardinal Mage before her fortieth birthday. Gods knew I never would have.

She held her defense up and said to Xavier, "Is this true?"

"It is, Samana. It is. I agreed to this meeting as a Friend of the Duke," Xavier said in his high-pitched, annoying voice. "And I was alerted to Mandeight's presence in the city last night, though I'm disappointed to find him in such good company," he said, with a brief, judgmental glance to Basil. Basil responded with a slight lift of his chin making him seem even more pompous and snooty.

Sanama let down her defensive wards with a stomp of her foot, sending the Forces harmlessly into the earth.

"Brother," I said, giving Xavier a sidelong glance. I didn't get up.

"Brother," he said with a formal nod. I noted he had a slight smile on his face, and it looked sincere. He'd probably be practicing his duplicity whilst in the Duke's court.

Basil had pushed two tables together with six chairs. Three different wines had been decanted, along with pale and brown ales. Two loaves of warm bread sat on the table as well.

"Cardinal Mage Xavier," Basil said, nodding to a chair. He approached and sat down. He sat opposite me and we stared at each other briefly.

Basil held out a second chair, saying, "Cardinal Mage Samana." She sat down as he adjusted her chair.

Basil sat down where the two tables had been pushed together. He had arranged the seating so that I sat at one end and my brother at the other. Jass and Kidal sat to my right and left, and Samana sat to Xavier's right.

He dutifully poured wine for each guest, not asking for preferences, as it appeared that he knew them already.

He sliced the bread into thick chunks and set each slice on plates he'd set before us. Butter and a selection of jams were placed strategically, so everyone had easy access to whatever they liked.

Samana pointed to a small bowl of jam.

"Is this dulapnaberry?" she asked of Basil.

"It is, Cardinal Mage. I remember that you were fond of it when you were apprentice to the last Cardinal Mage of the East, and I was head butler."

She gave him a genuine smile and said, "thank you, Turnwell. Should I still call you Turnwell?"

"I wish that you would. It reminds me of days when I was younger," Basil said smiling.

There were no such pleasantries between me and Xavier. We only briefly glanced at each other, more to make sure the other wasn't looking. A few times we accidentally made eye contact. We both looked away quickly.

Finally, Basil straightened himself and spoke.

"I brought you here, Cardinal Mages, to convey information of critical importance to the duchy and His Grace, Duke Elkis of Eldemy. As I know that Master Mandeight is considered an exile, I would ask that his apprentice, Jass of Ecota Isle, convey this information," Basil said.

"You dare to take an apprentice?" Samana spat. She looked at me with disdain.

Her words and manner truly wounded me. I had known Samana at the Collegium. In fact, she had been quite kind to me before my expulsion. I'd actually grown rather smitten with her. She still wore her black hair short, which I'd always liked, and in truth, I still found myself somewhat smitten.

That kindness of youth was gone though. She clearly saw me as a threat, or at least a scofflaw.

As a stared at her, I barely noticed that Jass looked panicked, staring first at me and then Basil.

"There is no Collegium on Ecota Isle, Cardinal Mage Samana, and she is a significant talent," I said formally. Samana gave me a searing look, and Xavier only barely shook his head in an all-to-familiar expression of judgment.

I continued: "She discovered much of this information herself and lost a family member to the dark mage in question."

"No doubt it was you," Samana muttered.

"That's not true, my lady," Jass said in my defense. The personal attack on me seemed to bolster her resolve.

"Cardinal Mage Samana is not a noble. No mages can hold noble titles, Young Mistress Jass. Her correct form of address is Cardinal Mage," Basil corrected gently.

"Thank you, Master Basil," she said formally. She seemed to feel only a bit chided by Basil's words. Basil considered proper etiquette of utmost importance. His years as head butler had honed his ability to correct etiquette without causing embarrassment. It was a skill few outside of the ducal household would possess.

What followed made me prouder of my apprentice than I could have ever imagined. She set out the information she discovered in the archives at the Governor's Mansion on Ecota Isle. Then she recited, word-for-word, the notes I had written many years ago about Marwoleth. She then conveyed the information Kidal had given us about Marwoleth and the Duke's Pride. She left out no detail and made no errors. It was as if her mind captured information and stored it precisely as she had received it.

When my twit of a brother Xavier, or Samana, asked questions, she answered them completely or simply said she didn't know the answer.

"But, Apprentice Jass, we have no proof that the mage who set the traps on Ecotal Isle is this Marwoleth," Samana said. She had used the appellation, apprentice, which indicated that she did not consider her a mere child, or the assistant of an unpatented mage.

"We do not, Cardinal Mage. But this mage did use at least two heretofore unknown Forces in his enchantment of the stones," Jass answered. "Master Mandeight. Did you bring the stone?"

"I did, Jass," I said, producing the stone from my purse.

I set it on the table, exposing the two runes of the unknown Forces.

Both Xavier and Samana gasped, though they tried to conceal it.

I eyed them both, though they tried to avoid my gaze.

"Clearly by your reaction, you at least recognize these runes," Jass said. Well done, Jass, I thought.

"We do, Apprentice Jass. We do," admitted Xavier. His expression was sad, no doubt because he would have to concede that I was right and to be believed.

"I would ask you two, you most respected Cardinal Mages, is not one of these runes connected to the horrors of the mage that Kidal spoke of?" Jass pressed. She was speaking of Marwoleth's magic that turned drowned sailors into the undead.

I was so proud. I knew nothing of Jass's past, but it was clear that she sure knew how to present an argument.

"One of them is, Apprentice Jass," Xavier said. "The second rune represents the Force of undeath."

I raised my eyebrows and gave my brother a scandalous glance. He averted his eyes. I was the black sheep of the family, the one who was expelled and exiled, and I didn't know, though I could guess, what the runes represented. Good student and all-around suck-up Xavier recognized the rune of a dark Force on sight. Someone was going to have some explaining to do.

"Then even if the mage who wrought these stones is not the Marwoleth of old, is he, or she, not a dangerous necromancer?" she asked.

Checkmate, I thought.

"Well," started Xavier, "we would have to examine the enchantment."

"There is no enchantment," I interrupted, "I broke it myself."

Xavier scowled at me. At least I thought it was a scowl. I returned it in kind, actually doubly so.

"But you recognize the runes without examining them, Cardinal Mage Xavier Birdstaff," Jass said.

I concealed a smile.

"You are correct, Apprentice Jass," Samana said, resting her hand lightly on Xavier's. "And I also recognize the other rune. It is most dangerous and powerful. It represents the Force of space and time. It is one of the God Forces."

I looked at Samana with surprise. So, the God Forces are real, I thought, and Samana knows of them enough to speak with authority. That was very interesting.

"It seems that the Cardinal Mages know of things that would scandalize even the highest Masters of the Collegium," I said.

"We are familiar for academic reasons," Xavier answered coldly.

While the Cardinal Mages were mages of significant power and political authority, they answered to a much higher authority, at least magically speaking.

All patented mages owed allegiance to the Masters of the Collegium. These were mages who eschewed political position and power. They lived magic. They obsessed over the knowledge of magic. They were wise beyond any level a working mage could ever hope to attain. Some called them mage-saints. They were the teachers of all of us, and they did not brook dark magic, nor magic that would shatter the very fabric of reality.

When those in the halls of power originally drafted the laws that created the Patents of Magic, the Masters of the Collegium insisted that only they would have the right to grant and rescind those patents. This gave them considerable power over all mages, even long after they graduated from the Collegium.

"What would Master Abias think," I wondered, "if he knew his most prized students were so familiar with such dark and evil knowledge," I said aloud with feigned curiosity.

Both Xavier and Samana looked at me flatly. I only smiled back.

Jass continued her line of thought.

"Clearly these runes represent most dangerous Forces, Cardinal Mages," she continued. "And both of the runes appear in Marwoleth's signatures in the records on Ecota Isle. If this is not Marwoleth, then perhaps it is one of his apprentices. And should we not seek to stop such an apprentice?"

"You may be right, Apprentice Jass," Samana said, looking significantly at Xavier. "Allow us to consult with our fellow Cardinal Mages. One is not here, but we expect him back shortly."

I made an effort not to glance at either Jass or Kidal, and I hoped they were doing the same. Any slim chance of this plan working would be axed if they found out their missing Cardinal Mage, Basma, had been killed by pirates and that we had helped.

Clearly, no one betrayed anything, as Xavier continued. I breathed a small sigh of relief.

"We will need to take the stone as proof," he said quickly snatching it up.

"No problem," I said, "I've already copied down the runes."

Both Samana and Xavier frowned at me.

"For academic reasons, of course," I added with a syrupy smile. "Though, should you refuse, I would like it back to continue tracking our necromancer."

"You tracked him from this stone?" Samana said with a whisper. She again looked at Xavier.

"Yes," I replied.

"You do realize that there are … ways of backtracking such scrying," she said.

"Only if he's ready for it," I replied. I was actually rather good at scrying. Apart from air magic, it was one of the few things I took to without much effort.

"How do you know he wasn't, dear brother," Xavier said with an air of superiority.

"Calculated risk," I said.

"Yes, you've made several of those, haven't you?" he said. It was more of a statement than a question.

I replied with yet another smile. My cheeks were becoming sore from all the smiling.

"I did a second scrying this morning," I announced. "It appears he's holed up in the Wall Mountains, almost directly to the Northwest. I can fetch my map to give a more precise location.

"Let's not get ahead of ourselves," Samana interrupted. "We don't yet know if we will be involved." She finished her slice of bread, drained her cup and stood. Xavier followed suit.

Samana left without a word, and I thought Xavier would do the same, but he stopped for a moment at the door to the Bonny Scarecrow and turned.

"Master Turnwell, Apprentice Jass, Master Kidal," he said, then looking at me said, "Mandeight."

I thought he was just snubbing by dropping the honorific, but then he said something that floored me.

"It is good to see you," he said to me, "good to see that you are well." Then he turned to walk away, only to stop again.

"Mother, she asks after you. You should write her. Or visit her whilst you're here," he said.

"I will, if I'm not arrested," I said dryly.

"I doubt that will happen. I'm not at liberty to say much, but the information you conveyed here is ..." he searched for the right words, "consistent with other events we've noted of late. The duke is mustering an army currently, though it's not yet public knowledge."

"Mandeight!" Samana called from the street. He turned and left.

We sat there for a moment, while I reeled over Xavier's words of kindness and his revelation. I wondered if they were sincere, or if he was lulling me into a false sense of security. Either could be the case, but if an army was mustering, that was significant.

"Now that wasn't so bad, was it, Mandeight?" Basil said interrupting my train of thought.

"No thanks to Mandeight's tongue," Jass spat.

I was still thinking about the Duke raising his army, but then I realized what Jass had said.

"Now see here, apprentice," I began.

"She's right," Kidal said with finality. "If we're going to do this, we'll need their help. And we'll have to work together, without the bickering," he added.

"Thank you Kidal," Jass said. "Now please excuse me," she said standing up. Basil quickly stood to hold her chair, but she was already headed toward the stairs. "Don't bother Basil, I'm not a real lady." I thought I detected the sound of sobs as she quickly climbed the stairs.

"Well done," Kidal said darkly.

"I do hope she's not thinking she will find her mother alive when you find this necromancer," Basil said refilling our cups.

"Is that even a possibility," Kidal asked.

"That's very doubtful," I mused. "If they're right about that enchanted stone, it means that it not only transported her but did something to her having to do with the Force of undeath."

"Maybe that's just to prepare her for something?" Kidal proposed.

"Possibly, but it's been years since she was taken. Whatever he was going to do with her, he certainly would have done it by now," I answered.

"What do you know about her parents," Basil asked.

"Nothing whatsoever. All I know is that her mother was taken when she was very young. She knows nothing of her father. Perhaps she never knew him, or he, her. Who knows? Her given name might be a bastardization of her actual name. Why do you ask?" I said.

"Maybe nothing, but she's awfully well-spoken for an orphan. Especially an outer islander," Basil replied. "She speaks as if she received at least some formal education."

"Not much of that on Ecota Isle," I said.

"Perhaps that's not where she's from," Kidal guessed.

"You may be right," I said.

It was strange that Jass was so well-spoken. She had practically dazzled Xavier and Samana. I'd certainly not taught her anything about rhetoric or language. That was all her, and she was good at it.

In fact, few commoners had such a command of the language or logic. And she spoke with two people of great authority with comfort. That, too, was remarkable. Clearly, she was more than a simple outer isle waif.

"Regardless of all that, you mustn't get her hopes up about finding her mother. In fact, I suspect you may need to lower her expectations," Basil said.

"She's never mentioned to me any hope of finding her mother alive and well," I said.

"Maybe that's because she doesn't want to hear whatever answer you may give her on the subject," Basil said.

I thought back to my first meeting with Jass. I had mentioned that it was unlikely she was alive, but I had couched that statement in kindness. Maybe that wasn't a kindness, maybe it was my own reluctance to give her extremely unpleasant news.

"And you certainly wouldn't be gentle about it," Kidal added.

I began to protest, but I saw his point. My previous experience in Eldemy had turned me bitter, no doubt. I was neither circumspect nor diplomatic. Apart from witty quips, I was rather direct.

CHAPTER FOURTEEN

When the page arrived from Duke Elkis' palace, I was shocked, to say the least. He wore the Duke's livery. He was formal, almost smug when he arrived at the Bonny Scarecrow.

When he walked in, he very formally handed a note to Basil. He gave Basil a reverential bow, no doubt due to his former station. I doubt the lad was old enough to have worked under Basil, but someone had told him who Basil had once been.

The three of us were enjoying a dinner that Basil had called "the Gamesman's Feast." It consisted of rabbit, venison, goose and duck, all roasted with root vegetables, including onions, parsnips, carrots and turnips. And it was delicious.

The final dish, which remained untouched, was announced as fox pâté. Kidal looked sickened when the footman announced the dish.

"What's wrong, Kidal?" Jass asked almost immediately after the footman departed.

"Fox. It's too much like dog. You shouldn't eat dog. It's too noble of an animal to be food," he said looking queasy.

"How can you call a beast that spends its day licking its own arse noble?" I asked almost incredulous.

"It's not that. They're loyal. More loyal than most people I know," Kidal said simply.

None of us ate the fox pâté.

Basil approached our table with the note in hand.

"What's that?" Kidal asked.

"It's an invitation, for all of us, to attend a meeting of His Grace's privy council," he announced.

"What?" I said, dropping my fork.

"You heard me right. The good Cardinal Mages spoke with His Grace and conferred with the other viziers. His Grace has decided that you should join his privy council so they may ask additional questions about the matter at hand," he explained.

I looked at Jass, and she looked back, wide-eyed. We both turned to Basil, who bore a smug expression.

When I caught Jass's eye, I gave her a nod of praise.

"Well done, Jass," I said. She looked to be in shock.

"What should I wear? Is this alright," Kidal asked wryly.

"You wouldn't be expected to wear anything formal, given your station," Basil answered.

Kidal looked offended, but he shrugged and continued eating.

"They want us to help come up with a plan?" Jass asked in wonder.

"No," I quickly corrected her. "They want information. Once they have that, they may tell us to get on the next ship out of Eldemy, or they may arrest us."

"They may also ask you to help," Basil suggested. "And although you hold no Patents of Magic, they do know of your talent. At least Xavier and Samana do."

"I doubt that," I said with a frowning smirk.

It was the next morning when Basil hired a horse and wagon to take us to the palace. On the way, he gave us a brief but detailed primer on proper court etiquette, should we meet the Duke during our visit. Jass listened intently, as did I. Kidal feigned disinterest, but when Jass or I asked a question, Kidal listened to the answer.

A while later, I noticed that Kidal was looking at the ring on my finger.

"Why does that stone change color," he finally asked, interrupting Basil's etiquette lesson.

I held my hand up, examining the ring. It was slowly changing from a medium gray to a darker gray.

"It's the first thing I enchanted at the Collegium," I replied with a note of nostalgia.

"But what's it do?" Kidal asked.

"It's a simple tracking spell. Beneath the stone is a hair from an individual. It tells me how close they are," I explained.

"It can track Xavier!" Jass said, immediately jumping to the correct conclusion.

"Mandeight! How could you?" Basil said, somewhat offended.

I held up my palms in my own defense.

"I was but a child when I wrought it," I protested.

"But you still use it," Basil replied, with an accusatory glare.

"Well, I wear it, and check it from time to time," I said with a smile.

"That is very impolite," Basil said.

"Well, you don't have a sibling wanting to put you in jail," I retorted.

Basil ignored that, and we continued the ride to the Duke's palace in silence.

When we arrived at Duke Elkis' palace, I was awestruck by the grandeur of it. I'd only ever seen the palace from afar.

It was made of a white stone that was mined and barged from High Fall thousands of years ago.

The outer walls of the palace stood forty-eight feet high, according to Basil. They were topped with stone carvings of dragons, all of which looked down on us lowly mortals. The outer gates were made of iron reinforced stonewood, which was harvested from the trees of an ancient forest that lay far inland and to the North. Not far from where I suspected Marwoleth might be holed up, I noted.

As our wagon approached, the doors swung outward, no doubt using some unseen mechanism within. The courtyard was laid with stone tiles, thick enough to withstand the weight of the many wagons and carriages that passed over it.

The palace proper was made from the same stone, with four turrets standing nearly 100 feet high. I could spy guardsmen patrolling the battlements on the turrets and in between. A lone butler, dressed in the white and gold livery of the duke, stood before the open doors to the castle. They too were wrought from the same stonewood and were also reinforced with black iron.

As the wagon stopped, the butler approached Basil and gave him a slight bow. Basil returned it. They had a brief conversation that none of us could overhear. From what I'd heard, you learned to whisper well when you were part of a noble household.

The butler led us into the castle, through a large and extremely grand entryway. There were paintings of notable dukes, and shields bearing the sigils of literally hundreds of former rulers.

Within the entryway, I felt the gravity of nearly ten thousand years of history. I didn't count them, but I knew there were four hundred and thirty-four shields displayed within the entryway, each representing the reign of a single duke. One for each duke of the Elkis line, a line that had remained unbroken for four hundred and thirty-four generations. Each time a duke died, the eldest male descendant of that duke had taken his father's place.

Within each portrait, I could see familial traits: a strong chin, a large, regal nose and wise, studying eyes.

The history of the Old Empire was fragmented and long faded to time, but no dynasty of that ancient empire had lasted this long.

I stood in wonder as I saw this visual representation of the longest dynasty to ever exist. It was humbling and terrifying. How could a single family successfully rule the Sovereign Duchy of

Eldemy for nearly ten thousand years?

It made my mind reel, and it gave me hope.

If the Marwoleth we were dealing with was the same one from the siege of Eldemy, he was almost three thousand years old. The Elkis dynasty was more than three times that age. If that dynasty had not been usurped by Marwoleth, it was very likely the oldest dynasty in history.

That fact gave me a level of comfort I had not felt since before I had met Jass and before I knew there was a three-thousand-year-old necromancer stalking the shadows of our world.

Among the hundreds of shields, there was a small, unadorned door on the right wall. The butler opened it and beckoned us to enter.

We entered a small room with a large table dominating the center. Chairs surrounded the room, but they were pushed against the wall to allow free movement around the large table.

"Master Turnwell, former head butler to His Grace, Masters Mandeight and Kidal and Apprentice Jass," the butler announced as he held the door for us to enter.

Xavier was here, as well as Samana, in addition to an older man in the uniform of a soldier. I didn't recognize his insignia, but he was very high up in the military hierarchy.

Xavier made introductions. The older man was Lord Field Marshal Thuror Bramstone. It turns out he was about as high as one can get in the military. I had heard of him but never met him before. He had served as field marshal for both the current duke and his father.

"I apologize that the rest of the privy council is not here. They are making other arrangements, also regarding the matter at hand," Xavier said.

As I had suspected, this meeting was strictly one to gain information, as was obvious by Field Marshal Bramstone's constant barrage of questions.

He was particularly interested in hearing what Kidal had to say about the Duke's Pride and the events following her destruction. He never asked the name of the ship Kidal was on when they encountered the Duke's Pride, which was fortunate. Piracy was a capital crime. Perhaps the aging field marshal suspected but didn't want to let legalities get in the way of gathering much-needed intelligence.

After nearly an hour of interrogation, Xavier finally said, "Perhaps we should tell Mandeight and his companions of their part in this."

"Perhaps we should," the old field marshal said. "But first, I would have you trace, upon this map if you would, the direction of your last scrying of this dark mage."

I first pulled out my own map, which was remarkably similar to the one on the table, but less detailed. I consulted it and picked up two small stone markers that resembled chess pieces. I placed one near the area of the Bonny Scarecrow and the other in the Sea of Sand, a great desert that extended far beyond the Wall Mountains.

Then I picked up a small spool of thread and twisted one end around the first marker, extending the thread to the second. Then I looked at the field marshal. He was furiously writing in a large leather journal, making note of landmarks and coordinate markers on the map.

He wrote for some time. Finally, Xavier said with a clearing of his throat, "Field Marshal."

"Oh yes, my apologies. We need a second scrying from a good distance to triangulate the position," Field Marshall Bramstone said.

"If you have the stone," I said to Xavier, "I can do that now."

"No," the field marshal interrupted. "It needs to be from a far greater distance."

He pointed to the map.

"Up here, I should think. By Ecoja Smurt," he said.

"What?" I asked.

"The Lord Field Marshal is used to working with mages. He's worked with many. He knows that what he asks is an inconvenience, but if he requires it, it is not without reason," Samana chided, not so gently.

"I'm sure his reasons are sound, but…" I started. Then I realized what he was doing. With two lines of a scry, he would have a point of intersection, and the further away the second line was from the first, the more accurate the point of intersection would be. It was an application of scrying magic I had never considered.

I looked at the field marshal with an impressed expression. He gave me a small, but weary, smile.

"You know your stuff, Field Marshal," I said.

"Lord Field Marshal," Basil quickly corrected.

"Sorry, Lord Field Marshal," I amended.

"Not to worry. I've been doing this for a long time, and I've found that those with talents often don't recognize their full usefulness," he said giving me a stare with clear blue eyes, encircled by wrinkles.

"How will I get the information to you?" I asked.

Xavier produced two brass cups from his purse. They were polished to the point that they appeared to be made of gold. They weren't ornate, but simply smooth brass cups.

"You'll speak the location into this cup," he said handing me one. "I shall hear it in this one. Keep repeating the location until I confirm that I have received it."

I put the cup in my own purse, and Xavier put the other one is his.

"Cardinal mages, I would like to speak with Master Mandeight privately, if I may," the field marshal said.

Everyone – Xavier, Samana, Jass, Kidal and Basil – looked at each other with surprise. I joined in as well. Why would this old battle horse want to talk with me privately?

Then they all slowly walked out of the room.

The field marshal walked to the door and closed it, and I took time to examine the man.

He was tall, half-a-head taller than I. He had once been a strong man, but age had withered him.

He wore a red uniform tunic, with two gold braids on each shoulder. There were emblems on the epaulets that probably denoted his rank. Unlike many senior officers, he wore no ribbons or medals, though he had no doubt earned many. He wore tan riding breeches and black leather riding boots that came up to the knee. A wide black leather belt was wrapped around his tunic, giving his form the illusion of a broad chest and a narrow waist.

His hair was white and sparse. His face tanned with decades of exposure to the sun. His blue eyes were surrounded by wrinkles, as was his mouth, around which he wore a neatly trimmed mustache and beard.

"How are your scry walls, Master Mandeight?" he asked as he walked back to his place opposite me.

"No one's caught me yet," I said.

He smiled. "Good. Can you lay one upon this room? I don't want us overheard," he said.

I did so. It took me about ten minutes to do it, as I discovered the whole room was rife with enchantments – no doubt other scry walls placed by Xavier and his peers.

Once I finished, I said, "That should do it. Now, what's so secret?"

"You are going to play the part of a contingency plan, I'm afraid," he started. "The walls of this palace have ears, and I have suspicions that our necromancer might be listening. You're quite sure your scrywalls are secure."

"Absolutely. It's probably the stonewood doors. This place is teeming with them, and they come from a forest not far from where he might be," I said indicating the Stonewood Forest near where my line had intersected the Wall Mountains.

"Is that possible?" he asked with horror.

"Normally, I would say it wasn't, but we're dealing with a mage who may have been practicing for three millennia. I couldn't guess at what he's capable of," I admitted.

"Very well," he said sitting down. He motioned for me to join him, so I sat down at a chair next to him.

"I'm going to send three people with you to Ecoja Smurt," he started. "Two infantrymen, they're quite experienced and talented, and an assassin."

"An assassin?" I exclaimed.

"Yes. Our patrols have spotted what looks like an army near the Wall Mountains directly to the East, and possibly a large one," the field marshal explained. "My army is assembling twenty miles east of the city.

"We're assuming he's going to attempt another siege of the city, but we want to meet that army in open battle before that and disrupt his plans.

"Once we get the location from you, we'll march on him, if need be, but I don't think our travel will go unobserved or unmolested."

Xavier had mentioned that the duke was mustering an army. This was it.

"And what are we and your infantrymen and assassin to do?" I asked.

"I expect, if we're engaged by the necromancer's army, that his attention will be diverted toward us. I want you and my team to be ready to head to his position. If we are in fact held up by his army, I want you to get my team as close to the necromancer as possible. They'll take it from there," he said.

"You trust me to do this?" I asked carefully.

"I didn't until I spoke with Xavier, quite frankly. He says you're quite capable and motivated to put an end to this dark mage. He said you risked much coming here," he explained.

And I was floored again. Xavier, my twit of a brother, had talked me up to the field marshal? Not only that, but he said I was worthy of this man's trust. I didn't know what to think.

"I understand," I lied. "When can I tell my companions?"

"I wouldn't mention anything until you get to Ecoja Smurt, or at least far away from here. It will just be the six of you, and I trust my team entirely," he said.

"Even the assassin?" I asked wryly.

He smiled again. "Yes. Even her."

"You realize his army will be largely undead?" I asked. "Not to tell you your business, but I don't think that will be like going up against a living army."

He smiled again, but there was no mirth in it.

"I have been studying the writings of Lord Field Marshal Fielan Burke. He commanded both the defenses of the city and the army that broke the siege. He had a lot to say about it, and he seemed to keep very detailed notes. I have a good idea what we're up against," the field marshal replied.

"And old Fielan had neither cannon nor musket at his disposal. I do," he said smiling again. "I've studied Fielan's actions, both the smart ones and his mistakes."

"No doubt Marwoleth has been doing the same," I said cautiously.

Suddenly the old field marshal looked twice his age.

"That is true," Field Marshal Bramstone sighed. "But there's no help for it. We are the ones who stand at the precipice of history now. This is our battle, whether we want it or not."

The old field marshal's words struck me like a rock to the head.

This man had been the highest officer for more than a generation. He'd battled nomads from the Sea of Sand, Northman incursions into Ecoja Smurt and even one Southerner invasion. He'd won them all.

Now he seemed resigned to his fate, whatever that might be.

I began to wonder about Cardinal Mage Basma. Basma was the preeminent battlemage of the duchy. He had escorted Bramstone on most of his campaigns and probably played a pivotal role in each.

What had I done when I helped the crew of the Scarab take the Duchess Adina? What had I done when I changed the dynamics of that sea battle, which resulted in Basma's death? Had I unwittingly killed Field Marshal Bramstone's most valuable asset and weapon? Would his army have a chance without the duchy's most powerful battlemage?

Basma's body was now languishing on Tremble Isle, or perhaps making its way to Eldemy aboard another ship.

I wanted to ask Bramstone about it. Did he know Basma was overdue? Were his battle plans relying on Basma's presence? But I couldn't ask those questions. That would implicate me and surely result in my arrest or execution.

I kept my mouth shut and felt ashamed in doing so.

"I imagine the great makers of history often go to their fates reluctantly. To do otherwise would be madness," I said trying to assuage my guilt and reassure the aging field marshal.

Bramstone laughed, and it was a sincere laugh.

"That is very true, Master Mage," he said. "Let's hope history is kind to us."

CHAPTER FIFTEEN

By the time I had prepared Kidal and Jass for the trip north, they had grown suspicious of me, as they knew I was hiding something.

While the fact that I suggested we all secure cold-weather clothing didn't cause any suspicion, my suggestion that Kidal procured flintlock pistols and the required accouterments did. He eyed me suspiciously when he agreed to the errand.

He returned hours later with five pistols, a small pouch of lead balls, a few ingots of led, a ball mold and a small cask of gunpowder.

As flintlocks were quite a new development in the world of weapons, they were quite expensive. I had tapped my line of credit with Basil to pay for them.

As collateral, I gave Basil the location of my cottage on Lovers' Isle and told him how to find it and open the door. Not giving too many details, I told him there was an item of great value there, and if I didn't make it back, he could have it, also requesting that the rest go to Jass, should she survive.

I also wrote out a will, leaving all of my possessions on Ecota Isle to Jass. I gave it to Basil, and he took it gravely.

"So, there is a chance you won't return," Basil said to me in his small office.

"Oh yes," I replied. "I don't think any part of this will go well."

Basil looked at me, searching my face for some clue of what I was hiding.

I was hiding the fact that I had indirectly killed the Duke's most powerful military asset, Basma, but apparently, I hid the fact well.

"If it goes very badly, I will instruct Jass to return here. She can help you find the cottage on Lovers' Isle. You'll need to give her my will. She will need to present it to Abigail Blackstone. She is my landlady on Ecota Isle. Jass can handle everything there," I said grimly.

Basil nodded.

"You know," Basil started, "when I helped you escape those many years ago, I never thought I'd see you again."

"Neither did I," I said, smiling. "We never know where fate may take us."

Basil looked out his small window for a moment. Then he said, "the folk out here know about the assembling army. They're not stupid. They've seen companies of soldiers leave and not return. The Lord Field Marshal dispatched them subtly, but that only conceals so much."

"That is to be expected," I said.

"This won't be like the last siege. Back then, Eldemy barely extended beyond the city walls. Now, there are probably three or four times the number of people living outside of the walls as live within them," Basil mused. "A siege today will cost tens of thousands of lives."

"I know," I said. "And I'm sure the Lord Field Marshal knows it as well. He's going to try to cut off their path to the city."

"But if he fails," Basil began.

"I know," I said.

Jass, Kidal and I waited just outside the northern gates of the city for our escorts, which I didn't mention until we got there.

The northern gates of the city of Eldemy were as imposing as the rest. The wall was made of the same white stone, looming far over us. The gates were made of that nearly impenetrable ironwood, and they were reinforced with the same black iron.

Merchant trains, made up of dozens of wagons and men-at-arms, passed us as we lingered outside the gates. At this early hour, most of the traffic was heading out of the city.

We stood just off the road so as not to hinder the mass of outbound traffic.

"Who are we waiting for?" Kidal demanded. He was very suspicious now. He had discerned that I was hiding something, and he didn't like it.

"The Lord Field Marshal wanted to send escorts with us, in case there's any trouble," I explained.

"Uh-huh," Kidal said. He gave Jass a significant look, and she returned it. I was becoming exasperated with their distrust. They knew that I had a private meeting with the Lord Field Marshal. That much had not been a secret.

They also knew that the Lord Field Marshal didn't want to say what he was going to say in front of other members of the privy council. That alone should have conveyed the delicacy of our discussion.

"Look," I finally said, "I can't tell you everything until we're well-clear of Eldemy. It has to be that way. My apologies, but you'll understand once you know."

Kidal looked angry. Jass just looked hurt. I had trusted her will all kinds of secrets of the magical arts. No doubt she felt I should trust her with this, but I was unswayed. If Marwoleth could tap into the stonewood used in the palace, and much of the construction of the outer wall gates, I just couldn't risk it.

And I certainly didn't want to share my suspicion about the stonewood within earshot of the stuff.

I saw our escort approaching: two older men and a young

woman.

The two men appeared to be brothers, no, twins. Though the years had aged them in different ways, I could tell that they had once looked identical. Both wore their hair long and tied into great gray tails. They were clean shaved, but one wore a massive scar across his nose and cheek.

One was dressed as a merchant and the other, the one with the scar, as a guard-for-hire.

Each wore a scabbard, and each had a pistol tucked in his belt. The one dressed as a guard also used a long rifle as a walking stick. He seemed to be walking with a rather pronounced limp.

The young woman was dressed in nondescript traveling clothes, including breeches, a loose-fitting tan shirt, but with a long, hooded cloak fastened around her neck. She was pretty, but not overly so, with her brown hair cropped short, almost spiky.

"We'll pick up horses at a stable just down the road. We'll make introductions once we're on our way north," the young woman said, clearly taking charge.

Kidal glanced at me through the side of his eyes, and he shook his head.

After we procured our horses, which the young woman paid for, we set off north toward Ecoja Smurt.

"I'm Dail," she said to break the silence. "The merchant, there, is Bosul, and his brother is Torum. He's the one with the scar. That's the easiest way to tell them apart."

The scarred one, Torum, eyed her darkly, but his brother smiled.

"Torum barely has the sense to get out of the way of an incoming sword stroke, as denoted by his face," Bosul joked.

"I'm still prettier than you," Torum responded.

I introduced my companions and myself, and we continued on.

"When are you going to share the big secret?" Kidal asked out of nowhere.

Dail scowled at him and said, "not yet, southerner. We need a couple days travel between us and Eldemy."

We rode on in silence.

Once the outbound traffic from Eldemy thinned out, I set to continuing Jass's training.

"Jass and I are going to fall behind for a while. She needs to practice her control of the Forces," I announced to my traveling companions.

"Well get well away, Master Mandeight. I do not wish to be within the blast radius of an apprentice's misfires," Torum said.

"True enough," added Bosul. "We used to be stationed near the Collegium. It's a wonder that place still stands with all the accidental explosions."

The two brothers laughed and began regaling Kidal with tales of the many apprentice mishaps they had witnessed.

Once we were at a safe distance, I had Jass recite each of the rhymes of the elemental Forces: earth, air, water and fire. We started with earth, as that was least likely to spook our horses.

"Do you remember the rhyme for the Force of earth?" I asked.

"Of course," she said reciting it mechanically and perfectly.

"Very good, Jass. Now to actually use the rhyme, you need to think upon each of the words. This is very important, as the words create a construct within your mind that will allow you to safely channel and shape the force to your intentions. It not just the words, but the effect the words have on your mind and thoughts. They are describing the symbol of the Force of earth. Note each word carefully and try to envision the symbol in your mind. Again please," I said.

She recited the rhyme again, but this time, a small cloud of dust appeared before her and fell upon her horse's head. The horse shook its head in protest.

I was impressed. It had taken me weeks of practice, and hundreds of attempts, at the Collegium to be able to create even a single spec of dirt. Jass created far more than that on her second try.

I had her try again but suggested she attempt to manifest the Force of earth off to the side, rather than over her poor mount's head. She did so. By her fifth attempt, she had produced a solid stone about the size of her fist.

I realized that earth magic might be her forte, as she was doing things with the Force of earth I could only manage after months of study.

We then moved on to the Force of air, which was my forte.

We started with the air rhyme described in my brother's book, and Jass took to it as quickly as she did the earth rhyme.

"Very good, Jass! You are certainly a quick study," I said. I was actually getting a bit jealous, and I silently chided myself for thinking that, but I was still annoyed.

"Now I'd like you to try a different air rhyme. I wrote this myself while at the Collegium," I said with a bit of pride. Then I slowly recited the rhyme to her.

She recited it back exactly, then recited it again with purpose. A breeze picked up and shot ahead of us, causing Dail's cloak to flutter over her head.

She, Torum and Bosul looked back and gave us ominous glares.

We slowed our mounts to give us more space.

"That works even better than Xavier's," Jass said. "Can we try fire now?"

"We're not working with fire on horseback. That's a great way to get thrown," I said. "Horses have to be trained to carry mages hurling battle magic, and I doubt that gelding has had much experience with that.

"I'm a little surprised it hasn't thrown you already," I muttered.

"What?" she asked.

"Horses tend to get rather skittish around the Forces, especially if they aren't tightly controlled," I explained.

"Now you tell me?" She gave me an accusatory glare.

"We need to use our time as efficiently as possible. And falling off a horse isn't that dangerous," I lied.

We set up camp near a rock formation a hundred yards from the road. Bosul and Torum patrolled the area and scanned the horizon in every direction. This took them most of the hour it took the rest of us to set up camp. After that, the two brothers disappeared. I heard reports of a rifle in the distance.

Kidal and I stood up in alarm, but Dail gave us a placating gesture and said, "it's fine. They're hunting."

We sat back down, and I tried to relax. It was then that I noticed that Dail was eyeing Kidal with an appraising look.

"Southerner. You any good with that dagger?" she asked as she stood. Many in Eldemy called those from south of High Fall southerners. It was often considered an insult, and Kidal appeared to know that.

"I'm not too bad," Kidal replied staring at her dangerously.

"Come on," she said as she walked away, "let's work up an appetite. No cutting though! Just a touch with the flat."

Kidal looked at me as he stood. "This won't take long," he said winking to me. I noticed as he walked away, that Kidal was saddle sore. His legs were spread apart at the knees and he walked with an exaggerated gate, protecting his chafed flesh.

We could hear the sounds of exertion and an occasional battle cry from Kidal when the twins arrived with a small wild calf.

"Well done," I said. "I was thinking we'd eat hard bread and cheese tonight!"

Torum looked at his brother and said flatly, "We don't travel like that. Think you can dry what we don't eat, mage? Save it for later?"

Once again, a non-practitioner had come up with a use for my talents I had not considered, not that I relished dehydrating leftovers for the whole trip.

"Of course," I said. "But I think my apprentice, Jass, should do it. She needs the practice, especially with fire."

Jass looked at me. "Yes," she said eagerly, "I can do it."

While Bosul and Torum skinned and dressed the calf, I went over the rhyme for the Forces of air and fire, explaining that the fire must be tightly controlled, as we were trying to dehydrate, rather than cook, the meat.

Bosul pulled a butcher's knife from the pack on his horse and began butchering the animal. He worked with quick, precise skill, cutting each major muscle from bone and sinew and slicing each into thin layers. He laid them over a rope tied between two trees.

Jass and I got up and walked toward the meat-laden rope.

"Now, I've never dehydrated anything with magic before. Actually seems like a rather mundane use for a miraculous talent, but it will be good practice, especially for your control," I said.

I tried my hand at it myself first, calling up the Force of air and reciting the rhyme for the Force of fire. I started out gently, but soon realized it would take hours to dry the meat. I pushed the air Force harder, creating a torrent of warming air. The first few cuts of meat were dried in about ten minutes, and I realized this could be exhausting work. I already felt my control begin to waver.

"Be careful, Jass. This is exhausting work. You'll need to balance fire and air. Give enough air to dry the meat quickly but watch your use of fire. No. Wait," I said. I gestured toward camp, where Torum and Bosul were stacking wood for a cook fire. "Go start that fire for them first. Let's see what you can do with fire before we set you loose on our meals for the next week."

"Don't bother with kindling," I called to the twins. I pointed to Jass. "Firestarter."

They both looked at me and backed far away from the stack of dried logs. There was genuine fear in their eyes. It seemed their tales about working near the Collegium were true.

"Go to, Jass," I urged my apprentice.

She walked over to the stack of logs and I heard her quietly mutter the fire rhyme. Nothing happened.

"Recite it with purpose, Jass. Think upon each and every word. Visualize the symbol. You've seen it. You know it. Let the rhyme fill in the details," I called to her.

I realized it would take Jass all night to dry all that meat, so I turned to dry another section while she worked to start the fire.

Then there was an explosion. I felt a blast of heat upon the back of my head.

When I turned back toward Jass, the remnants of a column of fire more than fifty feet high was dispersing into nothingness, but the stacked logs were now ablaze, burning with rapid fury.

Jass spun on her heels and stalked back toward me, a satisfied grin on her face.

Though I've never understood it, perhaps because I had struggled so much learning to control the Force of fire, some mages love walking away from fiery explosions, and Jass was one of those mages.

She walked slowly toward me her chin held high. Bosul and Torum were aghast staring at Jass with that same genuine fear.

I laughed.

"Well done, Jass! Well done!" I exclaimed.

She turned back toward the blaze, surveyed it for a bit and turned back to me nodding with satisfaction.

She grimaced as she got within earshot.

"I wasn't sure how much to use. That's a powerful Force!" she whispered.

I laughed again.

"Oh yes, it is. That's why battle mages use fire. It's extremely destructive and it's difficult to control. It's almost as if that Force doesn't want to be controlled," I said.

"But if you're going to make jerky and not charred meat, you'll need to control it a little better. Only let the tiniest bit out when you dry the meat. You'll feel the Force fighting you, and when you do, recite the rhyme in your mind, reinforce the image of the symbol. That will help you keep it at bay," I explained.

While Jass set about turning the thin fillets into jerky, Bosul put the calf's tenderloin on a spit and placed it over the fire.

"We eat well tonight!" he announced.

Torum returned from his pack with a skillet, in which he placed beef fat Bosul had trimmed from the calf. He then picked up a small canister of flour and sprinkled some in once the fat rendered.

"Excuse me ... Torum," I said, struggling to remember his name, "are you making a sauce?"

"No. A stew. Found some wild parsnips, and there's a sage bush back over that hillock," he said tossing a bundle of said parsnips to Bosul, who deftly skinned and chopped them into tiny, uniform cubes.

Bosul passed the chopped parsnips back to his brother on a flat wooden platter. Torum then scraped the cubed parsnips into the pan with the edge of a knife and began stirring it gently.

"Grab an onion from my pack," Torum said to his brother. "And maybe half a clove of garlic."

His brother did so, deftly dicing each and putting them in the pan. Without a word, Bosul got up and walked to the horses again, returning with a few small canisters.

"Don't skimp on the salt again," he said, handing the canisters to Torum.

"You wanna cook it?" Torum asked menacingly.

"Yes," Bosul replied simply.

"Well, it's not your turn, is it?" Torum said. "I'll salt it as I see fit."

I watched as Torum carefully sprinkled salt in the pan, along with other seasonings I didn't recognize. Then he tasted it, scowled at his brother and added more salt.

This back-and-forth went on for nearly an hour when Dail returned.

"I'm starved," she said slightly out of breath. "Is dinner ready?"

"Almost," said Bosul. Then he looked up as Kidal limped back, only visible when he neared the firelight, as the night had grown dark.

He was drenched with sweat, his shirt clinging to his chest. He was breathing heavily, in the way I would if I'd been forced to run a mile, uphill.

He seemed unable to catch his breath as he stumbled to his mount, whereupon he pulled a water skin and nearly drained it.

Bosul, Torum and Dail smiled to each other, but none said a word.

Kidal slumped down next to me, smelling of hard labor.

"I think I'm getting old," he said to me.

"You're not a gaffer yet, southerner. You did well, just need to concentrate more," Dail said as she filled a plate with slices of tenderloin and parsnip stew.

"That woman is like a demon with a knife. I've never seen anything like it. It's like she has four arms," Kidal panted. "Long blades next time," he called to her.

"Long blades tomorrow, it is, southerner," she called back.

"No, not tomorrow. Maybe two days. Maybe three," Kidal said.

Torum started laughing first. Then Bosul. Dail, to her credit, never laughed most likely to save Kidal the embarrassment.

I was now glad I hadn't told Kidal and Jess of our companions. Most assassins begin learning their trade soon after they learn to walk, and the first thing they learn is knife work. I doubted poor Kidal would fare any better with long blades, though.

"She's an assassin, isn't she?" Kidal said realization crossing his expression.

Dail looked to Bosul, who shrugged.

"You are correct, southerner," she said.

"And you let me spar with her knowing that?" he asked of me.

"I thought it would be good practice for you," I said with a chuckle.

"Then who are the other two?" Kidal demanded.

"We're members of the Duke's Guard," Torum answered.

"Okay," Kidal said. "I'll spar with one of you tomorrow." He got up and served himself a plate, and he brought one back for Jass. She thanked him and started in.

Bosul offered me a plate as well. The twins were good cooks!

Hell, they could have done it for a living. I could have filled myself on the parsnip stew alone, but they had roasted the tenderloin on a makeshift spit, and it was also heavily spiced and seasoned, and it was amazing.

Each bite of tenderloin melted in my mouth. I'm no culinary expert. I see eating as a necessity, but this was a meal that rivaled anything Basil served at the Bonny Scarecrow.

And my delight at my meal reached new heights as I combined cuts of the tenderloin with the parsnip stew. The twins had somehow seasoned and spiced each dish to compliment the other.

Combining the two dishes created something that was more flavorful and delicious than I would have thought possible.

"Where did you two learn to cook?" I asked with no small amount of wonder.

"Our mum," they said simultaneously.

"Well, gods bless her," I said. And I meant it. Basil's chef and the stolen cook aboard the Scarab would do well to take lessons from these old veterans.

The two brothers smirked at each other and ate quietly.

"It's too bad we didn't bring some tarragon," one said to the other.

"Yeah," said the other, "it might have saved this."

I wondered what the twins could create in a fully stocked kitchen. If the Duke knew what these two could do in a kitchen, I doubted he would ever have risked their lives in the guard.

Torum stood watch when we finally went to sleep. Everyone slept well, as both the exertion of the day's travel and our subsequent food comma left us exhausted.

To my surprise, Torum was still on watch when dawn's first light woke me, but he was no longer just watching. He was cooking. He'd taken the remains of the previous night's meal and combined them with some eggs to create a sort of quiche.

But when Torum handed me my plate (the others were still asleep), I noted there were various leaves mixed in with it.

"I went foraging before dawn," he explained though I hadn't actually asked the question. "I found some wild spinach and arugula. There's also a bit of basil."

Everyone else soon woke and enjoyed their breakfast. We struck camp, mounted our horses and continued our journey.

That morning I learned that it's possible to sleep on a horse, as Torum slept nearly the entirety of our next day's travel.

On the second night, just after we made camp, I told Jass and Kidal of the Lord Field Marshal's contingency plan, and how we were to escort the two soldiers and the assassin to Marwoleth's keep if the army was stalled.

"Wait," Kidal started first, "so we're to sneak in and kill this necromancer if he manages to stall an entire army? What in the world made you agree to this plan?"

I started to speak, but Dail interrupted me.

"It's not as foolhardy as it sounds, Kidal," she said, eschewing the term "southerner." Apparently, his knife play had impressed her.

"The necromancer will be distracted commanding his army, especially at such a distance," she explained.

"How can he command his army at all from that far away?" Kidal demanded.

"He can see what his undead see, and he can place commands in their rotting minds," she explained.

"Bah!" Kidal exclaimed gnawing on a piece of jerky.

"No, she's right. I imagine he would have to be able to do that.

When Marwoleth laid siege to Eldemy, he was never caught. It's possible that he wasn't even there," I said.

"Won't he have to at least see them?" Jass asked. "Wouldn't he have to create a link with each one? Because if one was put down, he'd need another to take over."

"That's true," I said giving her a nod of approval. "But we don't know the extent of the Force of undeath. Such abilities might come with the territory."

"They do," Dail said.

I looked at Dail, and her pretty face was expressionless. Even though she was not a mage, she seemed to know a lot about the Force of undeath.

"One day, Dail, you'll have to tell me why you know so much about necromancy," I said eyeing the assassin.

"What makes you think I'll ever have to tell you anything, mage?" she asked. It wasn't exactly a threat or a challenge. It was simply a question regarding the facts at hand, and the facts at hand were disturbing. How did an assassin know so much about necromancy?

I wondered if it was a result of briefings with Xavier and Samana, and if that was the case, the two Cardinal Mages had more than an academic knowledge of necromancy, which was even more disturbing.

"We'll need fresh mounts in Ecoja Smurt," Torum announced cutting the tension. "If we need to make that run to the East, we'll need new mounts and fast ones."

"How long will that trip take?" Kidal asked glumly.

Bosul tore off a piece of jerky and said, "With good mounts? Four or five days, if we travel light."

"How is this army going to last that long?" Kidal asked.

"They can last a long time, and if they do get stalled," Bosul said, "the Lord Field Marshal is good at delaying actions. He'll have them chasing him all over the steppes."

"And he's got field artillery," Torum added also chewing on dried meat. "The old man has been studying the records from Marwoleth's siege of Eldemy. He knows the tactics the city guard used to break the siege. They used catapults then, throwing chains fixed to rocks. I imagine chain shot fired from eight dozen 12-pounders will work nicely."

"How does he know where to move his army?" Jass asked.

"He has a good idea where the necromancer is hiding. He just wants Mandeight's second scrying to confirm it," Bosul said.

Bosul's statement struck me like an iron pan to the face. If the Lord Field Marshal knew where Marwoleth was, why was he sending me so far north?

"How much of this plan aren't you telling us?" I demanded. "Our necks are on the line too."

"The Lord Field Marshal told me exactly what I told you, and no more," Torum said flatly with the unquestioning tone of a lifelong soldier.

"We know enough to do our job," Torum said. "The old man always gives us that." The two of them raised cups and toasted "the old man."

"I don't know. It doesn't sound like we stand much of a chance," Kidal said.

"It'll be tough, but the Lord Field Marshal will be distracting his army, so we don't have to wade through that nightmare," Dail said. "I think we might have the easier of the two jobs."

"Never had to fight undead, thank the gods," Bosul said.

"I have," Kidal said.

Torum, Bosul and Dail looked at him with surprise.

"You have?" Torum asked.

"Yeah. It was on the far side of Ecota Isle," he started. Then he retold the tale of the Duke's Pride.

"How did you take them out?" Dail asked with professional curiosity.

"We didn't have proper weapons," Kidal started. "Even the crew lost their blades swimming to shore. All we had was driftwood."

"You bested undead two-to-one, or worse, with clubs?" Dail asked with disbelief.

"Only three of us survived, but yes," Kidal said. There was no pride in his voic, only the hollowness of trauma.

Jass's expression turned dark.

"Do you think that's what happened to my mother? Do you think she's part of his army?" she asked quietly. I didn't say anything, and I glanced at Kidal. He was staring at the ground, avoiding eye contact, lost in his own dark memories.

"He took your mother, apprentice?" Dail asked her voice filled with kindness.

She nodded. "Years ago," she said. "He'd set traps on our home island. She found one. She just disappeared. She was there walking down a trail, and the next moment, she was gone."

Dail looked at Jass with sad eyes, but she didn't say anything.

Torum took up the conversation. "I wouldn't get your hopes up, lass," he said gently. "That was likely her fate. I wouldn't give up all hope," he continued, then he stared her in the eye. "But it's unlikely she still lives."

Kidal and I exchanged guilty glances. We had both meant to have this conversation with her, but it was two strangers who did it instead, two strangers who told her the truth when we couldn't. I felt small and powerless. Here was I, capable of harnessing great powers to perform miracles, but I couldn't tell my apprentice as simple, honest, yet uncomfortable truth.

In truth, I was being a terrible mentor. Sure, I'd dutifully put her to work learning the art and craft of magic, but my responsibilities to her extended much further. I had to provide moral grounding, demonstrate by example, if not the limits of what we can do, the limits of what we should do.

And how was I to do that if I was too cowardly to tell her a harsh truth? True, Kidal couldn't seem to do it either, but I was her mentor, not he.

Jass looked at me with an expression I could not read. Was she thinking about Basma's death? And what had that whole affair taught her about when and where she should use magic?

I did not sleep well that night.

CHAPTER SIXTEEN

Ecoja Smurt is even more unpleasant a place than the name suggests. It's an ugly name and an even uglier place. I'm told its name is derived from the lost language the old Northmen used to speak. They say the name means "harsh hold" in that long-dead language, but no one really knew for certain.

Apart from being a cold, harsh, dangerous, violent and all-around terrible place, it's also the city where Xavier and I were born, and our mother still lived here.

I had decided the day prior that I would take a few hours to visit with her, for I would receive no end of grief if Xavier found out I had come here and didn't visit her.

I decided to take Jass with me, so she could see my humble beginnings.

The farm where I grew up looked much the same as it did when I left for the Collegium when I was sixteen.

All the land up here was harsh and hard to farm, but a few tough nuts attempted to do so anyway, and among those nuts were my mother and father. Father had taken ill and died when I was only six, and my brother and I worked as farmhands until we each showed magical talent and were recruited into the Collegium.

After I left (my brother having been recruited more than a decade before), my mother had to hire hands to work the farm. This greatly reduced the profitability of the farm, but it looked like things had been well-maintained in spite of the loss of revenue.

The old farmhouse was made of stone and plaster. The old thatch roof had been replaced with wood shingles and appeared to be in good order. Much to my surprise, there was a new structure near the old barn: a workers' barracks. It looked large enough to house four workers, perhaps more.

I could see workers in the field, harvesting root vegetables: carrots, parsnips and turnips, I guessed.

The farm where I was born was far outside the walls of the city proper, though the city was within sight. There were four fields, each almost an acre in size. Two were left fallow to replenish the vital nutrients of the soil. The other two were planted. One was ready for harvest, and that's where the farmhands labored. The other showed small sprouts of plants that would be ready for harvest in a few months.

Jass and I approached the farmhouse and I knocked on the door.

"Oh, bless it! I'll be right there," I heard my mother say. Her voice was older, certainly, but I still recognized it.

She opened the door, and much of what I remembered still held true: she was plump and short, with a broad smile that grew even broader as she recognized me. I had missed the years when her hair turned gray, and it was now almost a pale, brittle yellow. The wrinkles and sags of her face and chin weren't there when I had left. She looked ancient. Gods, had I really been gone that long?

"Mandeight?" she said, not sure she was looking at her youngest son.

"Hello, mother," I replied with a smile. I was almost in tears. It had been so long since I had seen my mother, the woman who gave me the precious gift of life, the woman who had raised me and taught me and scolded me when I was bad.

I was then put upon with a fierce, strong hug around my midsection, as I was more than a foot taller than she. It felt good, though I was taller now than when I had last hugged my mother. I wrapped my arms gently around her and returned the hug.

We held each other for a long time, and I relished it, embracing this strong but kind woman.

She pulled me into the farmhouse and sat me down at the table in a flourish of tears and excitement. The house looked much the same on the inside as well, though much to my surprise it looked smaller. I had seen so much of the world after I left. The house was clean, well-organized and warm. Through much of my youth, this room had been my respite from the cold of the northern lands and those cursed fields.

"Oh, bless the gods that you've finally come home!" she exclaimed, unable – or unwilling – to contain her joy.

"It's good to see you mother," I said, having regained my composure.

Jass looked at me with a small, warm smile. Then she looked at my mother, trying to discern what parts of her features I had inherited.

Then she grew sad, realizing she would have no such reunion with her own mother. I placed my hand on Jass's, and we exchanged a knowing look. I nodded to her as kindly as I could, holding back the tears of this reunion.

I cleared my throat. "This is my apprentice, Jass," I said by way of introduction.

"Oh! And apprentice! You're moving up, aren't you, Mandeight?" she proclaimed.

"Well, I get on," I said.

"Soon you'll be a Cardinal Mage like your brother," she gushed, then she set off to make tea.

Jass looked at me with incredulity. She'd worked out another truth. I had never informed my mother that I had been expelled from the Collegium, and apparently, Xavier hadn't found the time to do so either. If she didn't know that, she also didn't know I'd been banished from the Sovereign Duchy of Eldemy altogether.

I looked at Jass and sort of rolled my eyes and shrugged. She gave me a wide-eyed, insistent glare.

"You never told her you were exiled?" she hissed.

"I hardly had the time," I hissed back, "I was running for my life."

"I made some biscuits yesterday, Mandeight. Your favorite: bitterberry," my mother called from across the room. "The gods must have known you were coming and whispered to me whilst I cooked."

She crossed the room and sat a plate of bitterberry biscuits on the table, saying, "the tea is almost ready."

"You've got to tell her," Jass pressed in a whisper.

"No! There's no point to it," I replied.

My mother returned a few minutes later with cups of tea.

We sat and drank tea and munched on biscuits in blissful silence, all the while, Jass was gesturing with her eyes to break the news to my mother.

I broke the silent repartee with my own counterstroke: "Did you know that poor Jass is an orphan, mother?"

My mother replied with a pitiful sigh.

"It's true. Her mother was taken from her when Jass was but a small child. She was living on the land – and the kindness of others – when I found her. I believe she will be a very talented mage one day," I continued.

She placed her hands on Jass's hand and said, "you poor dear. Growing up without a mother is no way for a child to go through life, especially for one so young!"

"That's very kind of you, mistress," Jass replied.

"Oh, don't be so formal, dear," she said, then her eyes blinked in realization. "How about you call me grandma? Daughter of my youngest son, or close enough. I'll never see any other grandchildren, the gods know."

Jass smiled, but then she looked confused.

"Xavier doesn't have any children?" Jass asked.

"Oh no. And Mandeight won't give me any grandchildren either," my mother replied.

"Why is that?" Jass asked.

"Didn't Mandeight tell you?" she asked. Then she looked a bit embarrassed. "I suppose that's a conversation between you and Mandeight, dear. Have another biscuit."

My mother asked us to stay for dinner, but I told her we couldn't. When she pressed for a reason, I told her we were on a special mission for the Duke. This impressed her and filled her with even more pride.

Although we didn't stay for dinner, I did spend some time talking with her and catching up.

I managed to tell her I was living out on the outer isles. I said it was for research purposes, which wasn't entirely untrue.

She told me about the farm hands she had hired after I left, and how she had to fire several of them, and how several good ones left for better pay. She had managed to save enough money to buy the land from the baron of Ecoja Smurt, which meant she no longer had to pay him rent. This made her far more financially secure, which I found to be a great relief.

"I'm sorry I haven't been able to stay in touch, but Ecota Isle is very far and no longer part of the duchy. Couriers bound for Eldemy are rare, and those bound for Ecoja Smurt are well nigh unheard-of," I explained.

"Oh don't worry, dear," she said. "It's good enough that you're here now. I worry about my youngest baby!"

I gave her a weary smile. I was the "baby" of the family, though I was nearly in my fortieth year.

"And now that you're home, you can write again," she continued.

The bottom fell out of my stomach, as I realize there was a very real possibility that this might be the last time I would ever see my mother. I might have to confront a three-thousand-year-old necromancer, and the likelihood of me surviving that encounter was actually rather slim. I had to tell her that, at least.

"Mother," I started, "we're on a very dangerous mission. I cannot give you details, and I'm sure you understand why."

His face blanched, and she struggled to sit down in the chair without hitting the floor.

"What do you mean, Manny?" she said, using my childhood name.

"We're doing something for the Duke – for Eldemy, and I might not make it back," I started.

"Oh my," she said quietly.

"Xavier is also involved, though he is very far away, and part of a different ... front," I said, struggling to find the right word without divulging anything.

"Xavier too?" she whispered.

"You won't lose both of us, mother. That would be very unlikely, but it's possible you may lose one of us," I said, and I wasn't sure why I said it so flatly. I certainly didn't want her to worry, but I also didn't want her to not hear from one of us ever again and not know why.

"Is it really that dangerous?" she asked.

"It is mother," I admitted. "Xavier would want to spare you the worry, as would I, but we have to do what we're doing. It could mean the end of the duchy if we don't do it. I hope you can understand that."

She looked down at her half-full cup of tea, then she said, "I do understand. You are both important to the Duke, and you do important work, though neither of you can seem to tell me anything specific."

"Neither of us can say anything. We're sworn to secrecy, but if we don't do this, tens of thousands could die. Maybe more," I said.

Her mouth became a flat line.

"I do understand the mathematics of one mother grieving for a lost child versus ten thousand mothers grieving. I truly do, but why does it have to be me? Gods be damned, why does it have to be me?" she said with a shuddering sob.

I took her wrinkled, aged, yet still soft hand in mine. I felt the all-too-familiar warmth of her touch, and it gave me strength.

"You raised mages, mother, and while that brings pride, it does not come without cost," I said gently.

"Oh, Manny!" she said, holding back tears.

"I know, mother. I know," I said, holding back tears myself.

Jass excused herself, but she didn't escape a strong, fierce hug from my mother before she walked out.

"She seems to be a sweet girl," my mother said.

"She is. She's had a hard life, but it should get easier now," I said.

"Take care of her, and yourself," she said.

"I will mother."

"I love you."

"I love you, too."

I walked outside, closing the door behind me. I almost began sobbing, but then Jass accosted me.

"You're awful, Mandeight!" Jass said as we walked away from the farmhouse.

"I beg your pardon," I replied, blinking back tears.

"You lied to that nice old lady, who loves you so. You're awful," she said.

"What are you talking about?" I demanded.

"You didn't tell her you were expelled or exiled?" she demanded.

"I didn't lie. I omitted the truth. Besides, Xavier obviously came up with some story or another, and I don't know what it is. If I'd told her the truth, she would have been disappointed – not to mention the fact that she would know that Xavier had been lying to her for years," I said.

"And what's this she said about no children?" Jass pressed further. "More secrets you're hiding, no doubt."

"What?" I asked.

"She said neither you nor Xavier would have children. What's that about?" she demanded.

"Well, I didn't think you were old enough for it to be a concern," I said.

"Well you might as well tell me now," she said, as she stormed down the road to where our traveling companions waited.

"Mages are forbidden to marry – well, technically, we're forbidden to have children, but if you're not having children, there's no point in getting married," I said.

"What?" she shouted. "You didn't think that was something I might want to know? How young do you think I am? I'm nearly old enough to marry. When were you going to mention that? On my bloody wedding day?" Jass fumed.

"I've never done this before, Jass. I've never been a mentor to an apprentice. There are so many little details. I learned most of them at the Collegium. My mentor there told me some of it, sure, but most I learned in my studies," I said defensively.

She fumed for a bit before she spoke again: "So why can't mages have children?"

I sighed, then I explained.

"It can cause confluences if mages marry and procreate. Even more so if two mages marry," I explained.

"What's a confluence," she said impatiently.

"All mages, all known mages, are born from what we refer to as mundane parents, people with no magical talent. If a mage has a child, it's likely he or she will produce a more powerful mage, and if two mages procreate, they will produce a very powerful mage. And if those mages were to procreate, and so on, you'd end up with veritable gods walking the world. This makes non-mages very anxious," I said.

"So, no mages have children?" she pressed.

"None that we know of, at least," I said. "It's possible some have secret offspring somewhere, though if too many very talented new students present themselves to the Masters of the Collegium, they will certainly grow suspicious. Discovering the rule-breakers wouldn't be difficult. It's pretty simple magic to discover familial lines."

"Were there any? Any of these confluences?" she asked.

"I'm sure there have been. Certainly, before the days of Patents of Magic, it was probably quite common. Mages might have agreed to bring a confluence into the world. It could have been quite commonplace. They might even arrange for their offspring to marry other confluences. Before the patents were established, there were likely quite a few very powerful mages wandering the world, swaying the minds of nations, bending whole populations to their wills.

"That's likely one of the main reasons the patents were established. The mundanes governing Eldemy were tired of being dictated to by veritable gods," I said.

"It must have been awful then, for mundane people," she mused.

"I'm sure it was, occasionally. Hell, if you look at history books from centuries ago, before the patents, the names of great mages were commonplace in those pages. They were mentioned more often than dukes or kings. They set the course of history in those days," I said with a bit of sad nostalgia. No, I hadn't experienced those times, but what must it have been like to be mage whose power rivaled kings?

Jass eyed me suspiciously.

"Those don't sound like the good old days to me," she said flatly.

"I'm sure there was a downside," I said, avoiding her gaze.

"Is there anything else I need to know? Anything else you've failed to mention?" she asked.

"Nothing that comes to mind. If I had patents to consult, I could tell you for certain, but I don't. All those restrictions are spelled out in the patents," I said.

She was quiet for a while.

"I'm sorry for snapping, Mandeight. I know this can't be easy for you, but I appreciate you doing it," she said.

"That's good of you, Jass. Should I remember anything else, I will tell you at once. I promise," I replied.

"Do you think Xavier would let me read his patents? Or Samana? Or some other mage? I should like to know what I'm getting in to, without any more surprises," she said.

"That's possible. We could copy them down for reference. The Cardinal Mages would probably be relieved that my apprentice was taking an interest in earning her patents," I said dryly.

"No doubt," she said with a smile.

CHAPTER SEVENTEEN

Jass and I joined Kidal, Dail and the twins beyond the settlements to the East of Ecoja Smurt.

In our absence, they had procured fresh mounts and supplies. They waited for us at the base of a small rocky knoll.

"Jass said you'd need high ground. This seems to be about as high as it gets around here," Kidal said as we approached. Though he was now dressed in his cold-weather clothes, he was shivering. It would be another few months before the snows started, but the air was certainly growing cold, and he was not used to such climes.

"Yes, very good. Thank you, Jass," I said, preparing to again cast the scry upon Marwoleth's stone.

"Can I try the scrying?" Jass asked. "I've been reading up on the Forces of body and magic. I think I can do it."

"Not this time, Jass. It's too dangerous," I said.

"But I would practice the Forces a bit first," she said.

"It's not your command of the Forces that's in question, Jass. It's the target," I began. "Xavier and Samana were correct that Marwoleth could trace back a scry. Best let me handle it this time. I'll walk you through it later, with a less dangerous target."

She frowned, and I frowned back. Xavier and Samana had been correct: Marwoleth could trace my scry. If Jass put too much power in the scry, it would be rather easy for our foe to use that connection to pinpoint our location. By now he was preparing to engage the Lord Field Marshal's army, and he might well be looking for some kind of flanking maneuver.

"I'll need some help with this, if you all do not mind," I announced. The truth was, I had not considered Marwoleth tracing a scry until Xavier and Samana mentioned it. After all, I hadn't graduated, and I missed nearly three years of magical training and theory, but I was able to piece together why they were concerned.

This time, I would barely allow any of the Force of magic out, which would make it very difficult to trace, but it would also require help to get an accurate heading.

"Is this knoll on the map?" I asked.

"It is," answered Bosul.

"Good," I said. "I'll need three stakes, I should think. We'll place the first before I begin the scry. Once I cast the scry, someone will need to plant the second. You'll need to work fast, as the stone will only lift for a brief moment."

Torum walked over to a felled tree and snapped off a few thin branches. He handed two to his brother and ascended the knoll with the third. Then he hammered it into the ground at the highest point on the knoll. He straightened up and gave me an impatient gesture. I hurried up the knoll.

"Can you split the top of the stake, Torum?" I asked.

He pulled out his sword and pressed the blade against the top of the stake and pushed, splitting it down a few inches.

"Perfect. Thank you, Torum," I said.

I pulled the stone from my purse and tied a leather cord to it. I threaded the cord through the split in the stake. As I did this, the others followed me up to the top of the knoll.

"Bosul, please place the second stake exactly under the stone as it lifts up. It will only stay there for a moment, so you'll need to act quickly. And make sure you line up the top of the stake with the stone," I explained.

"Understood, mage," he said matter-of-factly. He knelt in front of me, holding the makeshift stake in one hand and a stone in the other.

I held the other end of the leather cord, so the Forces had a conduit to the stone, and I began summoning the Forces and casting the scry spell.

Though my eyes were closed, I heard the first stake creak as the stone attempted to find its original enchanter.

I heard Bosul pounding the second stake into the ground.

I opened my eyes and looked down. We now had two points creating a line.

I knelt down and looked from the top of the first stake to the second. There was no obvious landmark that lined up with the two stakes, but I could see where the winding road leading east from Ecoja Smurt intersected with my imaginary line.

"Can someone take the third stake and go out to that bend in the road?" I asked.

"Gods, you do things the hard way," Dail muttered as she approached the first stake.

She pulled a compass from her purse and placed it atop the first stake.

"Torum!" she called, "get out your map."

Torum pulled a large parchment from his purse and placed it on the ground. He also pulled a compass from his purse, placing it on the map. Then he rotated the map until he was satisfied.

"Ready, Dail," Torum said.

"It's a bit shy of eighty-six degrees," Dail said.

Torum produced a spool of thread from his purse and pulled out a length to hold against the map. Bosul walked over and picked up his compass, holding it over the map.

"I little to the left," Bosul said. "Not that much! Back to the right. Little more."

Torum held one end of the tread on the map, marking the knoll upon which we all stood. He moved the other in accordance with his brother's instructions until he said, "right there."

Torum stretched the thread and placed his other hand across the map. The thread almost exactly intersected a red wax X that someone had placed on the map. A second mark, stretching from the city of Eldemy to that same X, was already scrawled on the map.

"It's the old Watchcave," Torum said. "That's what the old man thought. Good place to mount an invasion from."

"Watchcave?" I asked.

"It's high up on Cordell Mountain. Someone carved an observation deck into the top of the mountain. Never been there. Only heard of it. It's hard to get to, I hear tell," Bosul explained.

I'd never heard of this Watchcave, nor Cordell Mountain. The hundreds, perhaps thousands, of mountains that made up the Wall Mountains had names, but I'd never bothered to learn any of them.

"Who is this 'someone?'" I asked. "Who exactly built this Watchcave?"

"Not sure," Bosul said. "The Lord Field Marshal said it was mentioned in some of the earliest writings of the Sovereign Duchy of Eldemy, back around the year 1000, but it was already there then, and long abandoned. Probably dates back to the Old Empire. The old man thinks generals from the Old Empire used it to watch for invading ships from the sea."

"How would that help?" Jass interrupted while looking at the map. She traced a line from the Watchcave to where the location of the Eldemy army was marked. "How far is that? A hundred miles? No one can see that far."

"I bit more than that, but you're correct: no one can see that far," Bosul said.

"Line of sight doesn't always have to mean within sight, especially if mages are doing the seeing," I said.

"They say there's some artifact from the days of the Old Empire up there," Dail said.

"An artifact?" both Jass and I said.

"Yeah. It's supposed to let you see great distances," Dail explained.

"Like a spyglass?" Kidal asked.

"I'm not sure," Dail admitted. "One of my ... order," she seemed to struggle to find the right word, "knows someone who went up there once. Says it's very old. And enchanted," she added.

I had an odd feeling. Throughout my entire life, I had never heard rumors of Empire-era artifacts, and now, within a fortnight, I'd collected one and heard rumor of another, in a place we might go to, no less. That was a strange coincidence.

I wondered if this information came from Xavier, rather than a member of her 'order.' That would make sense. The other Empire-era artifact, the mirror in my cottage on Lovers' Isle, had been in the possession of Cardinal Mage Basma.

During our meeting at the palace, we were given no information about how our account was consistent with other facts the Cardinal Mages had discovered. I didn't even know what the mirror did, or the orbs that went with it. Yes, Cardinal Mage Basma, the duchy's most senior war mage, was bringing the artifact from somewhere in the South to Eldemy, but to what end?

Perhaps it was preparation for the very assault that was about to commence.

Had Basma's death interfered with the assault on Marwoleth's army? Or his keep at the Watchcave? I began to wonder if things might have gone better if I'd just stayed in my rooms on Ecota Isle and not gotten involved.

"We've naval-gazed long enough," Torum announced. "You should get that information to Cardinal Mage Birdstaff."

"You're quite right," I said, pulling the brass cup from my purse.

I held it to my mouth and spoke loudly, "Xavier! Can you hear me?"

I repeated my address over and over, for nearly ten minutes.

"They may be having a hard time of it," Bosul said grimly. "They tried to wait for Cardinal Mage Basma, but his ship was overdue, so they had to go without him. Too bad. Master Basma is a formidable battle mage. Probably the best."

"I've never seen a mage so powerful on the battlefield," Torum agreed. "We served with him about ten years ago, during the last campaign against the Orcvitae."

I looked to Kidal, who returned the gaze. We, of course, knew where Cardinal Mage Basma was. He had been killed by the Scarab's first and only cannon volley against the Duchess Adina.

I hadn't lamented Basma's death when it happened, but I was now. At the end of my first year at the Collegium, the masters pulled aside the two students in our class who were most adept at fire magic. I'd learned later that they were made apprentices to Cardinal Mage Basma.

Basma was old then, and I shuddered to think how ancient and frail a man he had been when one of the Scarab's cannons struck him down.

The masters of the Collegium often mentioned Cardinal Mage Basma as 'the most powerful battle mage in written history.' Written history extended back about ten thousand years. If Marwoleth was three thousand years old, then Basma was the most powerful battle mage in more than three of Marwoleth's lifetimes.

While we didn't celebrate Basma's death, we certainly didn't mark it with the respect it deserved. He was a mage of historic significance, and likely a confluence. He was literally a legend within his own lifetime.

"I watched him turn the very ground upon which the Orcvitae vanguard stood into fire and boiling mud, almost lava," Torum said. "I've never seen a mage so powerful."

"And mayhap you shan't see his peer within this age," I said, glancing briefly at Jass. She looked away quickly.

During our journey north, I had begun to wonder if Jass was such a confluence. With each and every Force I tested her, she showed mastery within hours, and such mastery would take an ordinary apprentice months to attain. No one, not even Samana, picked up mastery of the Forces that quickly. I wondered if Basma had excelled that quickly when he was training at the Collegium fifty or more years ago.

I continued trying to hail Xavier in the brass cup.

Finally, the cacophony of an obvious battle erupted from the cup, so loud that all of us could hear it. To my horror, the voice that came through was not Xavier's. It was Samana.

"This is Samana. Xavier is down. Do you have the location?" she shouted over the clanging of metal, the thunder of cannon and the unsettling screams of wounded and terrified men.

"We do," I shouted. "It is the Watchcave on Cordell Mountain. How is Xavier? Will he live?"

"I will convey the message to the Lord Field Marshal," Samana replied, either not hearing or not deigning to answer my inquiry.

Then the battle sounds muffled and disappeared.

"That was quick," Bosul said, giving a significant glance to his brother.

"Quite right," Torum replied. "I'm glad I'm here and not there. For now at least."

"You think we should start heading out now? Not wait for orders?" Dail said seriously.

I glanced at Kidal, and his face was pure intensity. He, far more than I, was familiar with battle, and he heard the cacophony from the brass cup. From his expression, I gleaned that things were not going well for the Lord Field Marshal's army.

"This is going to go badly," he said ruefully.

"Well," I began, "it seems like we're going to get the order eventually. Might as well get a head start."

Torum stood. "Well, let's mount up and go, then."

Then Torum looked at me. "Take only what you think we'll need," he said. "Nothing extra. We need to ride fast and hard."

Without looking at her, I said to Jass, "take only food and water, Jass. Nothing else. We need to leave everything else."

"What of my book on Forces?" she protested.

"I've got some oilcloth," Bosul said. "If what you need to leave is truly dear, we can wrap it up and bury it."

She got up and started pulling things from her pack.

"I should suit up," Kidal said, heading toward his mount.

In less than an hour, we buried what we could not carry and were riding east.

"There's a town due east of here. If we ride fast, we should make it by nightfall," I said.

We all mounted up and began riding east toward a tiny village called Dex Majan.

CHAPTER EIGHTEEN

Our mounts from Ecoja Smurt were both well-rested and fast. The beasts carried us to Dex Majan a few hours before midnight.

It was a typical farming village. There was a temple to the gods favored by farmers and a mercantile store, where the locals could buy supplies imported from the city, including plow blades, seed and sundry wares one couldn't find in a place so remote.

Across the flatlands of this northern waste were a dozen humble farmhouses, each nestled among cultivated fields. Both moons were full this night, and the moons' light glistened on the dew-covered leaves of the crops, all low and squat.

I called to Dail, who was at the front of our column. "Dail! We need to slow," I said.

"Why?" she demanded.

"We'll spook the watchman," I replied. She slowed, and the rest followed suit.

There was a watchman on duty in a small shed by the road approaching Dex Majan. He lifted a lantern as we approached.

"Hail, travelers," he said, in a thick northerner accent.

Since I was from here, I took it upon myself to speak for the group.

"Hail and well met, watchman of Dex Majan. I be Mandeight Birdstaff, of Ecoja Smurt. My companions and I are on the Duke's business. We seek lodging for the night, and food and feed for our mounts, for we have rode hard," I said, allowing my own northerner accent to slip in.

"I didn't know you spoke bumpkin, mage," Dail whispered.

"You want to sleep on the dirt tonight?" I hissed. "Quiet, please."

"Birdstaff, you say?" the old man said. "Are you kin to Dalright Birdstaff?"

"I am his youngest son, in fact," I replied.

"Little Manny?" he exclaimed. "I haven't seen you since you were a young buck, all bragging about going off to magic school!"

"It has been quite some time," I replied.

"Manny," Kidal whispered. "Manny Birdpizzle." He and Jass stifled a laugh.

I closed my eyes and tried to ignore them.

"Well, come then," the watchman said. "I'll wake Godfir. He'll put you up and tend to your mounts."

We followed the watchman to the center of town, where he hammered incessantly on a door until Godfir answered.

He was rather angry when he opened the door, but when he was informed that "little Manny Birdstaff" was here, "and all growed up, and with fancy friends from the big city," he smiled, reluctantly, and let us in.

Godfir called three times to his stable boy, who eventually emerged from the stables and led our mounts away.

We were led to two rooms. Dail and Jass were put in one, and Kidal, Bosul, Torum and I were led to the other. I don't know how Jass and Dail fared, but our room was small, crowded and smelled of horse, sweat and road.

Before daybreak, Dail made the rounds and woke us. She had already roused the stable boy, and new mounts were saddled and ready to ride.

We left Dex Majan before anyone but the stable boy was up. Their reminisces with "little Manny Birdstaff" would have to wait for the return trip, if there was one.

By now, we could see a faint outline of Cordell Mountain. It was the tallest of the Wall Mountains in this region. The Wall Mountains separated the vast flatlands of Eldemy from the rest of the world to the East and South. They extended as far to the North as anyone dared venture and ran roughly parallel to the coastline until they reached the southern extent of the duchy, whereupon they made a sharp turn west, toward the sea.

Cordell Mountain stood high and magnificent on the dawn-drenched horizon. Even from here, its white, snowy cap shown brightly.

"We should have brought more winter clothes," Kidal grumbled.

"Something makes me think we won't be up there for long," Jass replied with ominous prescience.

"We don't have snow where I come from," Kidal said. "What's it like?"

"It's cold and wet," I replied.

"I've never seen snow either," Jass said.

Just then, Torum slowed his horse and joined us.

"Once we hit nightfall, we'll make camp. Then we need to discuss the plan," he said.

"How can we make plans until we've seen the place up close?" I asked.

"Dail drew up a map, with information from her acquaintance," he said, emphasizing the word "acquaintance."

"So, she knows even more about this than she's telling us. Great," I said.

"She's the one who's going to do the necromancer," Torum said. "I suspect she knows a lot more."

As we rode, I motioned to Torum to lag behind, so that I could talk with him privately. He did so.

"What do you know of our assassin?" I asked him.

"Nothing, except that the old man said she could be trusted," he said with finality.

That didn't satisfy me.

"You do realize that assassins are apolitical?" I started. "They work for money. They're mercenaries."

"I do," Torum replied. "But I also know that the Lord Field Marshal said she could be trusted," again saying the last phrase with the finality of a loyal and disciplined soldier.

"You will forgive me," I started, "but I do not hold the Lord Field Marshal's word with such reverence, nor did I hear it myself."

"I was but a young swain when I joined the guard," Torum began "The Lord Field Marshal was but a captain then and in charge of the Duke's guard. He's never lied to me, and he's never led me astray," Torum said. He smiled at me, and the scar across his nose and cheek puckered in a sickening display, but I could tell he was sincere.

"I hope the word and judgment of the Lord Field Marshal can be trusted," I said.

Torum pulled back on the reins of his mount, and his horse slowed. I followed suit, watching Jass, Dail, Kidal and Bosul ride even farther away.

"I will tell you this, mage," Torum started, "Lord Field Marshal Bramstone has never told me a single word that proved untrue. He looks upon each man under his command like a son, and if he confided in you, he would feel just such a familial bond."

I barely remembered my father, and except for the male

teachers at the Collegium, I had never had a father figure within memory.

Lord Field Marshal Bramstone had trusted me to create scry walls to block Marwoleth's attempts to eavesdrop, and he had done so without hesitation.

"The Lord Field Marshal had trusted me with secrets that I do not believe he shared with anyone else," I admitted.

"That's his way," Torum said. "He's a good judge of character. If he trusts you, I trust you, and if he trusts Dail, I trust her. So should you," he said with a level stare.

"Do you think his good judgment of character extends to mercenaries?" I asked.

"I do. We had several companies of southern mercenaries with us during the Orcvitea campaign, and he told our lieutenants which could be trusted and which could not. And he was never wrong," Torum said.

"Very well, Torum," I said. "I hope his sense of trust holds true."

"I will," Torum said simply.

Once nightfall came, we quickly made camp. We were still eating the calf jerky Jass had dried days before, along with hard bread and dried, cracked cheese. Once everyone's hunger was sated, Dail spoke.

"This is the closest thing I have to a map of the Watchcave," she said, producing a parchment from her purse. We all gathered around to get a look.

It was a hand-drawn map, and I instantly recognized the writing on it as Xavier's.

"This is from the friend of a member of your order," I said slyly.

"Quiet, mage," she snapped. She probably realized that I recognized Xavier's handwriting.

"There's a trailhead here," she indicated a point on the map. "It leads up the mountain with about two dozen switchbacks. Then the staircase starts."

"Staircase?" Bosul asked.

"Yeah. They're carved into the stone, and it's a long way up, my friend," she glanced at me menacingly. "My associate said it took nearly half a day to climb them. They lead to a flat spot near the top of the mountain on the desert side."

It was well known that the other side of the Wall Mountains was a vast desert, stretching hundreds, perhaps thousands, of miles to the East.

"That's where the entrance to the cave complex is," she said.

"Complex?" I asked, "I thought this was some sort of watchtower."

"It is," she replied, "but it must have been much more – once upon a time."

She pulled a second drawing from her purse, but this time, it wasn't made with Xavier's handwriting.

"The entrance to the complex is on the western edge of the flat. Once you're inside, there are two passages. The one to the right," she traced her finger along the roughly drawn map, "leads to a very large cavern. There's an opening in the northeastern side of the mountain, but it's not accessible from the paths or the staircase.

"If you go straight," she again traced a path, "it comes to a small chamber with an opening to the East. That's the observation platform. That's where the necromancer will probably be."

I began to speak, but Dail cut me off with a serious glare.

"Your job," she was speaking to Bosul and Torum, "is to get me to the entrance on the eastern flat.

"Mandeight," she said, turning to me, "I need you to escort me through the entrance and into the observation platform. There will probably be wards and such."

"Can I come?" Jass asked.

Dail looked at Jass and then me. "Only if your mentor agrees," Dail replied sharply.

"She sees magic far better than I," I said. "I think she would be of use."

Jass smiled at me. It was the first smile since she met my mother, and it gladdened me.

"Whatever you say, mage," Dail said. "Once the entryway between this passage and the observation deck is cleared, I move in and end the necromancer."

"Contingencies?" Bosul asked.

"If I fall, you or Torum must do the deed," Dail said simply.

"What if Mandeight falls?" Torum asked.

"Then it's up to Jass to clear the way, I suppose," Dail said. She looked at Jass, as did Torum and Bosul. Jass withered under their gazes.

"You'll do fine, Jass. Just go slow and be careful," I counseled.

"What if they both fall?" Bosul asked. Jass went wide-eyed.

Bosul noticed this and said, "I beg your pardon, young apprentice, but in such situations, we must consider all contingencies, even the most unpleasant, and unlikely."

Jass nodded.

"If that happens, we hope there aren't any wards, and we three move in to end this bastard," Dail replied.

"Hey, what about me?" Kidal asked.

"You're with Bosul and Torum," Dail said. "I suspect he'll have at least some undead up there. Someone will need to deal with them. You've already dealt with undead. If he has them in the passageway or the observation platform, you deal with them. Torum and Bosul can back you up."

"The last time I fought undead, it was tougher than any fight. Even with you," Kidal admitted.

"Kidal," Dail said seriously, "I've only met five fighters as well skilled with a blade as you, and four of them were in my order. You'll do fine."

Kidal raised his head with pride. Both Bosul and Torum eyed Kidal with appraisal. Our journey had been so hasty, that neither twin had spared with Kidal. They seemed to wonder if they should have tried the dark sailor when they had the chance.

"In two nights, we shall be at the trailhead," Torum said as he stood. "We should get to sleep. I'll wake everyone a few hours before dawn."

We slept, woke and rode another day. Then we repeated it again. By nightfall, we were at the base of Cordell Mountain.

I looked up at the improbable height of the mountain, looking for the opening that was the observation deck, but I could not spy it.

I noticed that Dail kept staring up at the same spot.

"We should make camp by that grove of trees," she said.

I agreed. Should Marwoleth look down with his ancient, enchanted spyglass, he would surely see us, even though we couldn't see him.

We made camp behind the trees, and it was quite a relief. Though I could not see the necromancer peering down at us, I could feel his presence, and it sickened me. I was dizzy and nauseated. Jass noted my aliment and helped me to sit down.

"Do you sense that, Jass?" I asked.

"Yes," she replied, "it's like a sickening smell, like that of burning human flesh, but I can't actually smell it."

I could see her holding down her dinner, and I rested a hand on hers.

"You don't have to do this, Jass," I said. "We can take care of it. If things go bad, you can send word to the Lord Field Marshal and make your way back to Basil. I've left instructions with him."

"No," she said with a slight smile. "I'll see this through." She looked up through the foliage of the trees, to the dappled image of the looming mountain and its snowy white cap.

"I know my mother won't be there, alive anyway. And I know you didn't want to tell me that," she started. "But if I can help end the man that killed her, that will be enough."

"It will have to be, Jass," I said. She nodded grimly.

CHAPTER NINETEEN

Again, we were awakened before dawn, but this time it was Bosul and Torum making the rounds.

"We'll leave the mounts here. Don't tie them. If we don't come back, they can go back to being wild horses. I'm sure they remember," Torum said, while scratching the muzzle of his mount.

Then he kissed his horse on its wet nose.

We left most of our camp intact, since we wouldn't need any of it, and started up the trail. It was steep and treacherous. Several times, we had to nearly cling to the mountainside to avoid sections where the trail had collapsed from erosion.

We followed the switchbacks, climbing ever higher until the trail led us around the mountain to its east side.

For the first time in my days, I saw the sight that was the Sea of Sand, the great desert that had separated Eldemy from the rest of the Old Empire. Ancient books said that the Sea of Sand was once a vast, lush valley of green farmlands, forests and meadows.

But that was no more. According to those ancient texts, this vast valley was ruthlessly burned to ash and stone by some magical or divine calamity. This happened, according to those texts, nearly ten thousand years ago, around the time of the fall of the Old Empire.

Some postulated that this calamity actually caused the fall of the Old Empire. Others suggested that this calamity cut Eldemy off from the rest of the Old Empire, for no one could travel the hundreds or thousand miles across the treacherous desert.

Regardless of the historical theories, it was a beautiful and ominous sight. The Sea of Sand was flat and nearly featureless, but for sand dunes that looked like enormous white and yellow waves. It was no wonder it was called a Sea of Sand, for it truly was an ocean of white and yellow, and it extended as far as I could see.

I could see massive dust clouds just on the edge of my vision, and I imagined that these winds changed and shaped the sand dunes.

I noted that the backside of Cordell Mountain, and the portions of the other mountains I could see, were still black and devoid of vegetation as if the mountains themselves shielded the Duchy of Eldemy from the terrible calamity that caused that vast desert.

"There used to be nomads there," Bosul said, huffing and puffing as he climbed the trail.

"Where?" I asked, barely able to speak from a lack of air.

He gestured to the vast desert. "Out there, tribes of nomads. Torum and I were in the company that repelled the last of them. That was a long time ago," he said almost sadly.

"That was our first real fight," Bosul added. "Who was that twit that led us?"

"Major Baskill," Torum said flatly.

"That was him! What a tool!" Bosul exclaimed as he stopped to catch his breath.

"You both survived. He must not have been that much of a tool," I interjected.

The brothers looked at each other, silently decided who would tell the story. However they decided it, Bosul spoke first.

"Major Baskill had been given orders to repel the nomads. They'd made incursions a ways south of here, raiding small villages along the western side of the mountain range," Bosul explained.

"Mostly logging villages," he added.

"Then Baskill got the bright idea to end the nomad incursions once and for all," Torum continued. "We had damn near a regiment of footmen, a thousand men, maybe more. The nomads would send raiding parties of less than a hundred men. It was over-kill."

"Once we repelled the nomads," Bosul picked up the narrative, "Major Baskill ordered us to give chase, which was stupid, as we didn't have enough water to follow them very far, but we did it. Orders and all.

"The nomads' settlement was only about six or eight miles from the mountains. He ordered us to slaughter them all. We did it, but not a man there was happy to do it," Bosul spat.

"We started back toward the mountain pass, but we lost the light, so we had to make camp," Bosul continued. "Half the men couldn't sleep – nightmares. A few offed themselves during the night. They probably couldn't get the slaughter of women and children from their minds, not that any of us could."

"On the way through the mountain pass, Major Baskill fell off a mountain trail. The fall killed him. Damn shame," said Torum dryly.

"Yeah, damn shame," Bosul added, each brother smiled to the other.

"It seems like a reasonable solution to an ongoing problem," I said.

They both scowled at me.

"It was a tribe of three hundred nomads trying to survive in a desert. Can you blame them for stealing what they needed?' Bosul asked.

"I can't imagine a harder life," Torum said. "But that's a lousy end to a troubled life."

"It is, certainly," I began, "but..."

"You weren't there, mage," Dail interjected, staring at me dangerously.

I said no more on the subject.

As the trail circumnavigated the mountain, we finally came upon the staircase. I could tell that the stairs had, in some long-forgotten millennium, been carefully carved from the stone. The remnants of runes and sigils, long rendered unreadable through the erosion of the ages, were visible on the sun, rain and wind ravaged stone.

I wondered at those fading runes and sigils. Were they part of some long-faded enchantment? Or were they tributes to the gods of the Old Empire? I took a moment to summon the Force of magic to examine them. What magic was left of the runes and sigils was but a faint shadow, but I could see the intention behind their workings. These markings were part of an enchantment, one to slow the erosion of the very stone into which they were carved. Whoever had built this watchcave had intended it to outlast the Old Empire, and they had done well with this working. While the stones showed erosion, they were still usable, and that was a testament to whoever carved them, and whoever enchanted them.

I wondered at the magical workings laid upon these stairs. Was there a mage living today who could work an enchantment that would last ten millennia? I certainly couldn't, and I doubted there was a mage alive who could make such a working last a century.

I thought of the mysterious mirror that Basma carried from the South (which now sat in my cottage on Lovers' Isle), and the enchanted glass orbs that went with it. Those workings were still strong and powerful, and they were likely as old as these stairs.

While historical accounts of mages in the Old Empire were rare and mostly unreadable, like most of the writings of that age, a few stories survived. Those old mages were truly formidable, capable of bending entire armies to their will and laying entire nations asunder.

What had happened to our kind? What caused our powers to be tamed? What caused the descendants of those near gods to become... ordinary? Was it the Patents of Magic? Even prior to the Conventions of Magic of 7420, few records survive of any mages whatsoever. Had they been purged? Did the mundane government of that era leave us neutered and spayed?

We began our ascension, which was exhausting. Bosul, Torum and I had to call for a rest several times. Bosul and Torum had the excuse that they were burdened with corslets and maille and that they were a decade or more older than I. I had no such excuse. I was simply unaccustomed to such exertion. While life on Ecota Isle was lonely and boring, it was comfortable, and I was paying for that comfort now.

At one point, Dail ran ahead. How she could run up those infernal stairs, I did not know.

She returned moments later.

"We're approaching the flat. We should let the Lord Field Marshal know we're here," she said, looking at me.

I pulled the brass cup from my purse and spoke into it again: "Samana! This is Mandeight. Are you there?"

There was nothing but silence.

"Try again," Dail pressed.

I did several times. All the while, Kidal was loading our pistols. The twins did the same with theirs, as well as their muskets. I ended up trying to reach Samana, or anyone on the other end, a dozen times or more, but we received no answer, no sounds of battle. Nothing.

I looked to Dail, Bosul and Torum.

"What say you? Do we press on?" I asked.

"No point waiting," Torum said. He looked up the rest of the stairs, trying to spot the entrance to the flat Dail had scouted.

"It didn't sound good last time," Bosul said.

"Agreed," Dail said.

"How far up is it?" I asked of Dail.

"Maybe eighty steps," she said. "Maybe a few more, but not bad."

"Give me time to catch my breath," I pleaded. "It's hard to wield magic when you're panting."

Dail gave me an exasperated glance, but she nodded agreement. She sat down and began sharpening a dagger on a whetstone. It was the same dagger she used to spar with Kidal.

We waited a quarter of an hour or less, but I felt rested enough.

We climbed the remaining steps. There were ninety-six, by the way, and we reached what Dail had called the flat. It was surrounded by cut rocks, creating a low wall around the flat area

Dail and Bosul took the lead, climbing the last few steps to the flat and bounding over, then I heard a hissing sound, and Bosul fell back into his brother's arms.

There was an arrow protruding from his chest.

Torum carefully laid his brother down and began to tend to him. Kidal slowly climbed the last few steps and peeked over the edge of the flat. He ducked back down just as another arrow hissed above his head.

"Dail is down too," Kidal whispered. "Two archers up on rocks above. Both to the left."

"About where?" I asked of Kidal.

He moved his hand to two positions, estimating the locations of the two archers.

"Would be nice to have a bowman right now," I muttered.

Kidal pulled a pistol and said, "Almost as good."

"Too loud," I replied, "We don't want to alert whoever's inside there."

Kidal gave me a shrug, saying "we go to war with what we have, not what we wish we had."

"Too right we do," Torum said, fury in his voice. His brother, Bosul, was clearly dead, as his lifeless eyes stared out at the unending sky, vacant and unfocused.

I stuck my head over the ledge and quickly withdrew. Two arrows flew over my head, but I had time enough to spot the two archers.

I muttered the rhyme of the Force of fire and summoned the Force of bolstering. I imagined in my mind two hair-thin shafts of fire emanating from my forefingers. I rose to stand and pointed a finger at each, unleashing the bolstered fire in shafts no thicker than the silk string we'd earlier used to mark lines on a map.

Each hit its target, though one had let loose an arrow, but its aim was off. In that brief moment, I realized the archers were undead, though freshly so. The skin of their faces was pallid, though not yet rotting.

I ducked back down and soon heard two loud thumps.

"Kidal," I hissed, "check to see if it's clear."

He did so.

"We're good. Both archers are down," he said.

I looked to Torum, who was cradling his dead brother.

"Torum," I whispered. "The mission. We have to go."

He looked at me, tears welling in his eyes, but he gave me a resolute nod. He blinked away the tears and stood, unsheathing his sword.

Kidal went first, climbing the last few steps in a wary crouch. Torum followed after him.

Once Torum gave us the all-clear, Jass and I climbed onto the flat. I saw Kidal checking Dail. She was alive, the arrow having only pierced her left shoulder. There wasn't much blood.

"We should take her back down and get the arrow out. We can

cauterize the wound," Kidal whispered.

"No," I said. "We don't have that kind of time. Our foe may have heard the undead fall, or he may have been alerted when they began firing. We have to move quickly."

Torum pulled Dail down off the flat and on to the stairs below. She winced, stifling a cry of pain.

She was awake, but her face was beaded with droplets of sweat. She was clearly in enormous pain. She tried to get up, but Kidal pushed her down, whispering something to her. She finally relaxed and nodded.

I moved up to the entrance to the Watchcave opposite the stairs and reached out while summoning the Force of magic. In doing so, I walked past the two undead archers. It turns out my aim was impeccable: both archers had pinholes in their foreheads, which smoked from my fire spell. I could see the Force of undeath emanating from their twice-dead corpses. The tendrils of magic spun into shadows of the Force's symbol. I took note of it.

Each of their corpses had broken apart on impact. Bits of them still twitched and wriggled. I turned back to the cave entrance.

There was a simple alerting ward at the entrance to the cave complex. I summoned the Force of lessening and began carefully dismantling the ward. It took me but a few minutes, but Kidal and Torum stood at the entrance on the balls of their feet, bouncing impatiently.

I nodded. The two moved in quickly but carefully, each man moving with practiced determination. They stopped at the first intersection. Jass stood behind me, her hand resting gently on my back. I looked back and she peered at Kidal and Torum as they signaled silently to each other.

Torum turned to us and motioned to stay back. Kidal slowly crept down a side passage to the right. On the map, this was the passage that led to the very large chamber.

Kidal emerged a few moments later and whispered, "all clear

there."

The passage winded to the left and then to the right, and as we made the last turn, we could see daylight emanating from the passageway beyond, where laid the observation platform.

I could see what looked like an enormous spyglass, perhaps ten or fifteen feet long. Its brass finish had turned dull with age, and it was mounted on a brass pedestal that was somehow fixed to the rock floor.

I reached out again, this time at a distance, and summoned the Force of magic again. There was nothing there, no ward, no enchantments at all, through the passageway, I could see magical tracings upon the gigantic spyglass. The threads of the enchantment were ancient and strong, though, without a closer look, I had no idea what they did.

Kidal crouched next to me, and I whispered to him, "there's nothing there. Now's the time."

Kidal nodded gravely. Then he turned to Torum and motioned toward the observation platform.

The two charged in. I followed quickly behind them, summoning the Forces of air and bolstering. While I couldn't burn the necromancer to death, I might be able to blow him off the platform. Gravity would do the rest.

The platform was empty. It was a large room, perhaps sixty feet wide and twenty feet deep.

There was a four-foot-high ledge separating the platform from what would be a fatal fall down the mountain. A similar ledge protruded from above, creating a long, circular viewing gap carved into the mountain itself.

The four of us stood near the spyglass and looked around. No one was there.

We stood for a moment, not believing what we were not seeing.

"Did we pick the wrong place?" I asked. "Maybe the map is off," I suggested.

"But what about the archers?" Kidal said.

"Maybe they're a diversion," I replied.

"Shh! Quite!" Torum hissed.

It was then that I heard the scuffling of dozens, perhaps hundreds, of feet, coming from the passageway behind us, the passageway we had just walked through.

CHAPTER TWENTY

Both Kidal and Torum spun and moved into position on either side of the entrance, to protect me and Jass. I could hear the scraping of boots upon the stone floor of the passageway, but it was loud, and I realized it was hundreds of boots.

The first undead that emerged from the passageway, the first undead I had actually ever seen close up, was a rotted, festering young man. He had probably only been in his late teens when he was turned. He wore a simple linen shirt and breeches, much like the clothes Xavier and I wore when we worked on the family farm.

I blasted him with a shaft of air, and he flew back into the passageway. He emerged moments later, impaled upon a pike, but he was still walking, and behind him was the first wave of undead.

This first wave carried pikes. I pulled Jass behind me as Torum and Kidal closed ranks to my left and right, just ahead of me. This left me a relatively clear view of the first wave of undead coming through the passageway.

The necromancer hadn't bothered to equip his soldiers with armor – only weapons. These walking corpses were much like the archers I'd seen before. They had the unmistakable pallor of death, their skin pale and almost green, being devoid of living blood.

They wore remnants of the clothes they wore in life: a butcher's apron, a merchant's robes, ordinary clothes you would see on people on an ordinary day in any town or city, but these clothes were tatters. They were torn and moldering, the seams having come undone long ago.

The Force of undeath must preserve the corpses, but not their clothes. They could be decades old, or more.

Most unsettling was the lack of sound. Sure, their feet made scraping noises as she shuffled along the stone floor, but I could hear no breathing, nor any sounds of exertion, no grunts, no battle cries, no groans, only the sound of shuffling feet.

I summoned the Force of bolstering and unleashed the Force of air, much in the same way I made the shield while aboard the Scarab, but this time, I directed the rock-hard air toward the passageway. I held my hands out before me and took a single determined step toward the undead and pushed with all my might.

I knocked the first two pikemen back into their undead comrades, causing an almost comical domino effect. The single undead vanguard we had first seen flailed helplessly as the pike upon which he was impaled as it rose and lifted him off the ground for a brief moment. Four or five ranks of undead fell, one rank after the next.

But this only slowed them down. Now that my view was clearer still, I could see that we were facing far more undead than the four of us could ever manage.

Kidal and Torum moved to either side of the passageway and began thrusting their swords into the prone, struggling undead. They impaled chests, heads, necks, causing a nauseating, blackened liquid to emerge from each wound.

But the undead pikemen showed no signs of injury. They kept struggling, trying to regain their footing. All the while, more undead, this time armed with swords, began climbing over, and trodding upon, their prone and struggling comrades.

My shield spell was able to stop their advance to a point, but soon more undead swordsmen began climbing over those stalled before them. Soon the whole passageway became a mass of dead, clambering post-humanity.

Kidal and Torum fought furiously, each slammed against the observation platform's rear wall by the edges of my spell. They cut and slash with speed and accuracy.

I noted that both Kidal and Torum were quite expert with a long blade. When ordinary wounds, which would cripple any living opponent, didn't work, they aimed for the head and neck.

Torum even managed to decapitate one pikeman, but the body kept moving, kept trying to stand.

"They're not dying," Torum shouted.

"Well, they are already dead," I shouted back, immediately regretting my witty quip.

My shield spell fluttered, and I regained my concentration, stabilizing it again. It was then that I realized that I couldn't hold this spell much longer. While mages expend no personal energy to cast spells, it is taxing on our minds. We must maintain images of the symbols within our minds to keep control of the Forces, and this can be mentally exhausting, especially for a sustained spell like this.

I had to make a choice: either end the spell or risk losing control of the Forces, which could be catastrophic.

It became clear that we were not going to win this day.

"Jass!" I shouted, "look over the edge. Can we escape?" I again felt my air shield waver and flutter. I concentrated again on the spell to stabilize it.

"It's a straight drop. Hundreds of feet. No way to climb down. It smooth, like a cliff face," Jass shouted back.

I looked back at her, and I began to lose control of my spell again, but this time I knew I couldn't control the Forces I had mustered. I ended the spell.

"Mandeight!" both Kidal and Torum shouted, now realizing my spell had failed.

I found it difficult to concentrate and looked about for another way to escape.

Jass stepped in front of me, loudly shouting the rhymes of the Force of fire. It was a rudimentary spell at best, but effective.

Fire, hot and fierce, rushed from Jass's outstretched palms. The blast toppled three or four ranks of undead and shot down the passageway.

Tendrils of flame curled and rebounded from the edges of the passageway, and Torum and Kidal quickly backpedaled to avoid being burned.

The flame was unfocused and diffuse, so it wasn't hot enough to ignite the flesh of the undead, but it was hot enough to ignite their clothing.

Row after row after row of undead warriors struggled to stand as their tattered clothing erupted into flames. Kidal and Torum cheered, as did I.

Then we realized that the undead didn't seem to notice they were being set aflame. They continued their advance, the sickeningly sweet smell of burning human flesh filling the observation platform.

The undead continued their advance, parting to the left and right of Jass' fire spell, forcing Kidal and Torum into their respective corners.

Then everything stopped.

Fire and smoke billowed through the passageway and onto the platform, but the undead stood motionless, slowly burning with hisses and pops.

Jass sagged back with exhaustion, and I caught her, holding her upright.

The air became thick with that sickening, sweet smoke. I began choking and coughing. Jass succumbed too, and I let her fall to the floor.

"There is no need for more bloodshed, friends," I young man's voice emerged from beyond the flame and smoke of the passageway. It was the voice of a northerner – perhaps someone from Ecoja Smurt, or further north.

Torum and Kidal continued hacking at the undead, occasionally knocking one down, but I could tell they were near exhaustion. Kidal was cursing with each blade strike. Torum was far more conservative with his efforts, his decades of warfare having taught him well.

"If you surrender peaceably, I will take you prisoner. You will be well-treated until your ransoms are paid, then I will release you. To that I give you my word," the voice said.

I looked down at Jass. She was sitting before me, panting with the strain of her rather impressive fire spell. Her face was a mask of hatred and terror.

I rested a hand on her shoulder. She shook her head. Clearly, she didn't want to surrender to this necromancer, the man who took and killed her mother.

I didn't want to do it either. If this necromancer's word was to be believed, which was doubtful, we would become pawns, interfering with the actions of the Lord Field Marshal and the Duke. What concessions would they have to make to gain our release? And would they be willing to make any concessions?

Worse still, what if the necromancer was lying. Would we end up footmen in his undead army, or worse?

I didn't know what to do, but I did know that I didn't want to die, and that prospect seemed imminent.

"Better to live to fight another day, Jass," I said.

Kidal and Torum must have shared the same sentiment, or they were just too exhausted to continue fighting. Though I could no longer see them through the mass of undead, I heard their swords clatter to the stone floor.

"Very good. Very good, my friends. I'm bringing forth minions with manacles. These are just a precaution until I know you are genuinely taking my bargain," the voice said.

We heard more shuffling and the quiet clanking of chains as the sea of undead parted.

CHAPTER TWENTY-ONE

While undead do smell foul, they only smell a bit like rotting flesh. More than anything, they smell like horrible body odor. Imagine a dozen laborers working day and night for months at a time, but they never bathe, and when they rest, the humidity shoots up, causing every mold, ever germ and every fungus to grow and flourish.

I do not know what body processes still worked within the undead, but some certainly worked. They were able to walk and fight. They were able to follow commands, though I do not know how our foe conveyed those commands, and all this would remain a mystery to me for some time.

Kidal had taken to breathing through his mouth, but I didn't think that tactic had worked well for him, as I could see sweat beading on his face, and he was swallowing saliva like a man preparing to vomit.

For myself, I kept my breathing shallow, and while I felt nauseated, I was able to manage.

Torum was not shy about expressing his displeasure of the stench. While he didn't speak, his grunting, huffing and gagging made it all-too-clear that he was not accustomed to such smells either.

Jass, on the other hand, was unfazed by the odor. Though her eyes were devoid of emotion, her mouth formed a line that indicated absolute hatred, but patience.

I had never in my life been manacled. Even when I was on the run after my exile, I manage to avoid capture.

I realized I don't like manacles.

First, there's the physical discomfort. Most of us don't realize how often we use our hands. We scratch our noses, even pick our noses, brush stray eyelashes out of our eyes, but when you've lost the use of your hands, you realize we are constantly itching and scratching ourselves like monkeys. Over time, this discomfort faded.

Then there's the actual discomfort of the manacles. In this case, our chains had been fastened to stakes set into the stone over our heads.

You try to hold your arms up, then your muscles get tired, and this happens alarmingly fast, so you let your arms hang, suspended by your manacled wrists. This, of course, causes the metal edges of the manacles to dig into your flesh.

Apparently, jailers, or the blacksmiths they employ, don't bother filing the burrs off of the cuffs, so you're fighting this constant battle of discomfort. One minute you're giving your wrists a rest by holding up your arms until your muscles start to cramp. Then you're feeling the metal cuffs gradually slicing and chafing your wrists. Of course, you try to reposition them, so the metal has fresh flesh to dig in to, giving your wounds a moment of respite.

But most disconcerting of all is the helplessness. More than anything, this is the real punishment of being immobilized.

Our arms and hands are our most natural tools of defense. We use them from an early age when play-fighting with our friends. We cross them over our chests when we're feeling defensive, whether from physical attack or emotional. We use them to shield our eyes when there's broken glass or bright light.

The psychological toll of being manacled cannot be overstated. It is, in its own way, torture.

The four of us hung from our arms in the very large cavern off the first turn in the passageway, the same cavern Kidal peeked into when we first entered the Watchcave complex.

Clearly, the necromancer had been concealing himself and his undead soldiers here, but Kidal didn't think to check for a company of undead and invisible soldiers. How could he have known? I hadn't thought of it, and I'm a mage.

As I stood there, trying to gain some small level of comfort, I tried to work out how he created that spell.

Many non-magical folk assume mages can make themselves invisible, but the fact is, I didn't know any mages who could do it, and I certainly couldn't myself.

Furthermore, I couldn't figure out how he'd done it. I suppose one could make oneself invisible to a single person, using the Force of mind. This would be like a personal illusion, and it would certainly be possible. It was something I would research should I survive this predicament.

But that's not what the necromancer did.

It made me wonder if there were more Forces of which I was not aware. Not god-like Forces, like space-time or undeath. No, there might simply be a Force of light.

I considered that it might be a specialized use of the Force of fire, but I realized, such a thing was beyond that Force. Fire was anxious and restless, and I imagined being invisible would take a far more serene spell. Though I didn't know fire well, I knew enough to know its limitations, and manipulating light itself was one of them.

But what if there was a Force that manipulated light?

Now, in hindsight, it seemed like a very logical hole in our repertoire as mages. We could use the Force of air to silence ourselves, though it required a delicate and fastidious touch to do so, but invisibility was another matter entirely.

It now seemed so natural for such a Force of light to exist, but the idea of it had never occurred to me until now.

While studying at the Collegium I had never even heard mention of such a Force, but it did make sense that it would exist.

Then the necromancer walked into the cavern, breaking my train of thought.

There had been four undead swordsmen standing near the cavern entrance, and as we heard his footsteps, they parted to make way.

As he walked in, I noted that he looked nothing like Kidal's description of Marwoleth.

He was short and rather stocky, and pale. His hair was long, bushy and fiery red, as was his long beard. In fact, he looked like many of the men I grew up knowing in Ecoja Smurt. He was definitely a northerner. He was a bit rotund but comfortable in his mage's robes, which were black with red accents.

"I know you were sent by the Duke. That much is obvious," he started. "I'm assuming you were his backup plan, yes?"

None of us answered. Jass, who was to my right, hissed something I couldn't quite understand, but it sounded like one of the Forces rhymes.

The necromancer took note of it as well and approached her. He was barely taller than Jass.

"You must be an apprentice mage," he said. She didn't answer, only staring at him with those emotionless eyes.

Then he looked down the line, first at me, then Kidal and finally Torum.

He took a step and stood before me, his hands behind his back. "And you must be the mage mentor, yes?" he asked.

I gave him a slight nod.

"Very good," he said. Then he walked before Kidal. "You are not of the Duke's army, are you?"

Kidal looked straight ahead with a stoic expression, remaining silent, though beads of sweat covered his head, and he swallowed frequently, but I didn't think that was due to fear. He was trying not to vomit, as it would inevitably end up all over his chest and stomach.

"I mercenary, perhaps?" he asked. "No, I don't think so. But you're good with a blade. Too good for a petty thief or typical bravo."

The necromancer wagged his finger at him, saying, "you're a mystery yet to be unraveled."

Then he stood before Torum.

Either Torum played a good game or the stench had so affected him that he couldn't even concentrate on what our foe said. He was simply ignoring him, and trying, like Kidal, not to vomit.

"Now you are a soldier. Definitely, one of two. Brothers, perhaps? We found your comrade dead on the stairway, I'm afraid," he said.

But there was no mention of Dail. She must have gotten far enough away to evade capture, or so I'd hoped.

"My name is Marwoleth," he said, walking away. "You may consider me your host. I've summoned a messenger to take my demands to your Duke, or his commander in the field. Can any of you tell me his name? He's certainly with that army my minions have been chasing around the steppes. I should like to address my message to the right man. Anyone?"

"Address it to the Lord Field Marshal," I said.

"I'm afraid I don't know the current Lord Field Marshal's name. I haven't kept up with current Eldemy politics. I remember Lord Field Marshal Brassade, but I'm sure he's long dead," Marwoleth said.

"He is. He died almost two centuries ago," I said. "The current field marshal is Bramstone."

"Not familiar with the name," he replied, smiling. "Thank you for your cooperation. The sooner he receives the message, the sooner you'll be freed."

And he left the cavern, the undead guards again parting the way for him.

Time dragged on.

Out of sheer boredom, I decided to examine my surroundings.

As Dail had mentioned, there was an enormous hole in the side of the mountain opening up this cavern to the sky. The floor of the cavern was littered with old bones. Some I recognized: cow's femurs and skulls, deer, and bear, I think.

But there was also what appeared to be human bones mixed in the clutter. Some were very old, as they'd turned the color of straw or wood.

There were larger bones as well, from animals I could not identify.

Then I noticed in the far corner, there was something, some sort of tall object a bit taller than me, that was covered with a large gray cloth. I summoned the Force of magic and reached out. I could sense the thin, intricate strands of that same old magic I'd sensed with the gigantic spyglass in the observation chamber and the mirror safely hidden in my cottage.

In fact, from the shape I could make out from the way the cloth fell, that might be one of those mirrors as well. It was too far away for me to see much of the enchantment, but it was very old and very strong, and it seemed strangely familiar, though I couldn't fathom why.

None of us dared speak of Dail, for we didn't know if Marwoleth could hear our whispers through the ears of our undead guards.

By nightfall, the stench of undead had faded. The four guards at the entrance managed to maintain a faint shadow of the smell, but now it just smelled like the trash heap behind a busy tavern, the food rotting slowly away.

CHAPTER TWENTY-TWO

I got no sleep that night. Every time I dozed off, my body slumped, causing the manacles to dig painfully into the now raw flesh of my wrists. The pain woke me immediately.

The only one of us who got any sleep was Jass, who was probably the only one light enough to manage it.

In the morning, we had the pleasure of being fed food and given water by Marwoleth's undead minions. It was a disgusting display I'd rather not describe. Suffice it to say, it was difficult keeping food down, and none of us ate or drank much. Just enough to stay alive, I suppose.

"The messenger is off. He should be there within the hour," Marwoleth said as he entered the cavern again.

He was followed by two dozen of his undead minions.

"Since you haven't tried anything, I will let some of you free, though you must stay here," he said. And without a spoken command or gesture, one of the undead approached Torum and unlocked his manacles with a large key hung around its neck.

It did the same for Kidal.

"I'm afraid I can't let you or your apprentice loose. I don't find soldiers without weapons much of a threat, but I can't say that for you or her," he said with a wan smile.

"No bother," I said with a bit of nonchalant bravado, "I would do the same."

"And your companions can feed you. My undead have many

uses, but I must admit, they make terrible household staff," Marwoleth said.

"We appreciate that," I said.

Marwoleth smiled at me again.

"I suspect, if your Lord Field Marshal is quick with his response, I should hear word in a few more hours," he said.

"That's quick travel for a messenger," I said.

"I've enhanced its speed," he replied.

I nodded with a colleague's approval.

"If the Lord Field Marshal doesn't meet your demands, what's to become of us?" Kidal asked while rubbing his wrists.

He smiled at Kidal, as if sizing him up, but he only looked at his eyes.

"Oh, that's a discussion for the future. No need to dwell on it now, is there?" Marwoleth replied. "Let's all hope he does."

"May I ask you a question, Marwoleth?" I started.

He looked at me with an expression of curiosity and surprise.

"I suppose," he said.

"I've been doing some research on you, or others with your name, I suppose. Are you the same Marwoleth who laid siege to Eldemy?" I asked.

He gave me a crooked smile.

"So, you've heard of me," he said with what I thought was genuine pride.

"So, you are one-in-the-same," I said. It wasn't a question. I decided to play on his pride. "I've read several contemporary accounts of the siege of Eldemy, and several works by historians in the subsequent centuries. From what I've read of the numbers, the placement of your troops, the siege engines that I assume you devised, I'm surprised it wasn't successful."

Marwoleth wagged his head about as if trying to think of the right words.

"Well, there are things about that siege that didn't make it into the history books, I'm afraid," he said.

"Really? Like what?" I asked. I was genuinely interested, and everything I'd mentioned about reading histories of the siege was true. That siege shouldn't have failed.

He smiled clearly not willing to tell me everything.

"I'll say this. The Duke had ... resources at his disposal of which I was not aware," he explained.

"Do you mean his tactics of using chains in his catapults?" I asked.

"No, though that didn't help my situation," he said. "He had a military asset. If you want to know more, try looking at historical writings outside of the Duchy of Eldemy. I think you'll find it interesting," he said with finality.

"So, you are indeed the same Marwoleth of said siege?" I asked to confirm.

His eyes narrowed, and he looked about as if trying to find a way to describe something extremely complex to a small child. I found it a bit insulting.

"In a manner of speaking, yes," he replied.

"So, you can change bodies? Transfer your spirit, your soul, into another body?" I asked.

"It's ... not exactly like that, but close enough for this discussion," he said.

"And you accomplish that using the Force of undeath?" I asked.

"Ah, an academic inquiry!" he exclaimed, smiling broadly. "Though I shouldn't be surprised by such a question from a fellow mage. And I'm not surprised a student of the Collegium would have inquiries about Forces forbidden by the very Patents of Magic you seek."

That confused me. I'd read Patents of Magic. All the students at the Collegium did. In fact, it was our first instruction, long before we started to learn to harness Forces.

The Patents of Magic, apart from giving a mage license to ply their art in the Sovereign Duchy of Eldemy, laid out a code of conduct for holders of the patents. There was an extensive and annoyingly complete list of things mages weren't allowed to do with their magic, but there was no prohibition of specific Forces.

I wondered if the negotiations between the government and the Masters of the Collegium had proscribed things that wouldn't be taught at the school.

Yet again, another thing I would have to research in historical records.

Marwoleth paced a bit and approached me. Two of his undead minions flanked him silently.

"This Force you call 'undeath' is actually far more encompassing than that name suggests. I think, in terms you would understand, it would be more the Force of the spirit or the soul," he said, waving his hands. "The two terms get conflated, but they are both part of the same."

"So these undead are," I started, "possessed by spirits?"

"Yes. I don't want to get too technical. Trade secrets and all that," he said. "But said Force is both flexible and useful, and before you ask, yes, it is used to enchant my minions and extend my life. It is one of the forces that turns mages into archmages."

That's a term I had never heard used seriously. Rival students at the Collegium would use the term with derision about a particularly studious apprentice. We would sometimes use the term to describe, in unflattering and ironic ways, the eldest and most distracted of the teachers there.

But I'd never heard anyone seriously call someone an archmage.

"You wouldn't be looking for an apprentice, would you?" I said.

"Mandeight!" Jass shouted, using my name as if it were a curse.

Her eyes were no longer expressionless. They were filled with anger.

Marwoleth let out a genuine guffaw.

"You're cheeky for someone chained to a wall! I like that. Unfortunately, I've learned that having apprentices can be dangerous business," Marwoleth said. "I made that mistake twice. Won't do it again."

Then he approached Jass, and he met her now hateful gaze.

"What's with you, young apprentice?" he asked.

"You killed my mother," she said.

"Did I?" he said with mild curiosity.

"Yes. One of your traps on Ecota Isle got her," she said.

"Yes. Those weren't very effective. Much better to place them in cities. They gave me a steady stream of bodies," he said smiling.

"I'm going to kill you," she said plainly.

He laughed dismissively.

"You should teach your apprentice humility," he said to me never breaking his gaze with Jass. "She'll have a short life otherwise."

Then he headed for the passageway and left, saying, "I must be off. I'll come back when my messenger returns."

Torum walked over to me with a ladle of water. I drank.

"Do you think he can listen in when he's gone?" Torum whispered.

"I imagine he can hear what his undead hear," I whispered.

He leaned in next to my left ear and whispered as quietly as he could.

"If I can get the key from that one," he said, "we can free you. Maybe we can escape through that hole." He looked at the large opening in the cavern.

Torum must have been whispering with Kidal earlier, because

Kidal was now strolling near said opening, stealing quick glances of what was beyond.

Then he turned to Torum and shook his head. That probably meant it was a dangerously sheer drop.

"I don't see how you can get the key without starting a row," I murmured. "And that would be bad, considering you're unarmed. Give me a minute to think."

And I thought. There were now eight undead minions here, all clustered around the passageway. Marwoleth must not have been concerned about an escape through the large opening, as he didn't bother to have his minions guard it.

I wracked my brain, trying to think of a way out of this when Jass hissed at me. I looked over and she was furiously gesturing with her head to something above me.

I looked up but saw only my manacled hands and stone.

"What?" I whispered. Torum looked between us, confused.

"Your ring," she hissed.

I looked up again, but this time, I twisted my wrist around.

She had been motioning to my ring, the ring that tracked Xavier, and the stone set into it was very nearly black.

CHAPTER TWENTY-THREE

I watched as the color of the stone in my ring shifted to pure black.

Xavier, my brother, whom I assumed was dead on a distant battlefield, was very near.

A horrific thought occurred to me: if Xavier had fallen, was he now one of Marwoleth's undead minions? I put that thought out of my head. Xavier was annoying, but he was also a very resourceful mage.

Then I heard faint scuffling from outside the large opening, and for just a brief moment, I saw Dail's head peek into the cavern and duck back down.

Kidal must have heard it too. He walked back to the opening and leaned against the wall, folding his arms. Though he wasn't looking at the opening, he appeared to be in concentration, as if listening. After a few moments he caught Torum's eye and gave him a very slight nod.

Dail must have whispered a plan to him.

Torum began moving indirectly toward the undead guards, and I realized he was going to attempt to grab the key.

Kidal was on the move as well. He walked midway between Jass and I and the passageway.

Then, moving faster than an old soldier should, Torum rushed the guards, grabbed the key, tore it free and threw it to Kidal.

All eight undead guards converged on Torum. One thrust at him with a short spear. Torum sidestepped the attack and grabbed onto the spear, twisting it and pulling it free from the guard's dead hands. One of its hands came right off with the spear.

Torum shook the wriggling hand off the spear and moved between the guards and us.

Just then, Dail bounded into the cavern. She unsheathed a short sword and tossed it to Kidal, who deftly caught it and joined Torum.

I could hear the sounds of more undead approaching from the passageway. As I had suspected, Marwoleth could hear, and possibly see, everything happening in the cavern.

I looked toward the passageway to the rest of the complex, expecting to see dozens of undead footmen begin marching into the cavern, but that's not what I saw.

I saw a blast of fire pass by the passageway, from the cave opening on the flat toward the observation deck. Unlike Jass's fire, this fire was white with flashes of blue, far more concentrated, far more destructive. The fire was fierce and sustained.

I could feel the blast of heat even against the opposite wall of the cavern. It was as if I had placed my face near a blacksmith's fire as he pumped the billows.

Undead minions rushed toward past the entryway toward the source of the fire, and they were incinerated nearly instantly, burning flesh and muscle sloughing off in fiery chunks. I could see the undead fall one after the other in a mass of gathering bones and burning flesh, but they kept coming.

Across the cavern, Dail pulled two daggers from behind her back and set upon the nearest undead guards. She dodged a spear thrust and spun behind the guard, crouching low and severing the tendons in the back of its ankles. The guard fell, unable to walk or stand.

Kidal kicked the guard nearest to him back, turned and began quickly unlocking Jass's manacles.

"Are you serious? You free the apprentice first?" I yelled.

Kidal just laughed. "Patience, my friend," he said, concentrating on the manacles.

Once Jass was freed, he started on my manacles.

"See, I am getting to you," he said with feigned placation, winking at me as he set my wrists free.

I couldn't see exactly what was happening, but Jass shouted, "Torum! Left!"

I saw Torum tumble free and Jass muttered the rhyme of the Force of fire.

Fire spewed toward three of the guards. Much like before, it wasn't concentrated enough to incinerate them, but it did knock them out into the passageway, where sustained white flame caught them and hurled them toward the observation deck.

Now I was free. During the time it took Kidal to free us, Dail had disabled two more of the guards. Only two remained, but they were now motionless, standing still and inanimate. Dail disabled them anyway, kicking their weapons across the cavern.

She ran to the passageway and yelled, "they're free!"

The rush of white-hot flame stopped as suddenly as it started, and a moment later, Jass ran out the passageway, toward the observation deck.

"Jass! No!" I shouted, running after her.

I was too late, for when I emerged into the hall, Jass had already disappeared into the observation platform.

I heard Marwoleth laugh and say something as I ran toward them.

Then I felt the hair on the back of my neck stand up, as I sensed the unbridled, totally unleashed Force of fire surround me and everything within the Watchcave complex.

"Gods! What is going on?" Xavier, the brother I had feared dead, shouted from behind me. He felt it too. It was a massive magical backlash, the kind of calamity that all mages feared. Whether it came from Jass or Marwoleth, I didn't know, but the very air within and around the Watchcave complex turned to fire. It was as if the very air turned flammable.

My lungs burned, as I didn't have the presence of mind to stop breathing. I fell to the ground.

Searing pain woke me as I coughed and hacked uncontrollably. Dail was patting me down, extinguishing my clothes. I sat up and wiped blood and spittle from my mouth.

Dail's hair was completely gone, including her eyebrows and eyelashes. Her skin was covered with a thin layer of soot, and her eyes were blood red. There was a trickle of blood coming from one nostril.

I got up and staggered to the observation platform. Jass laid singed and smoldering on the ground.

"Gods, no! Oh, Jass!" I croaked through my dry, burned throat.

I turned her over. She, too, was hairless now, and the left side of her face was badly burned.

Then she coughed, and I breathed a painful sigh of relief.

"I missed him. He jumped just as I was casting," she whispered, swallowing in pain at the effort.

I looked around the room. I didn't see Marwoleth, nor a pile of smoldering robes.

Kidal stumbled in, surveying the room, short sword in hand.

As he took in the scene, he marched to the ledge of the room and looked out down the mountain.

"Yup," he said. "We wouldn't have survived that fall."

Then he turned to us.

"He's down there, not moving, and there's a puddle of blood around his head." Kidal announced.

"Good," Jass said, laying back down and breathing carefully.

Dail walked in next. Her short hair had been very nearly singed completely off. She wore a grim, grief-filled expression, saying, "Torum didn't make it. Too badly burned."

Jass's face turned from relief to disbelief, from realization to horror.

"Oh no!" Jass whispered. "No! No! No! What did I do?" Then she began to sob, the effort causing her to cough convulsively.

I held on to her, as she became a pile of pain, remorse and regret.

Clearly, the calamity had come from her.

"It's not your fault," I lied. "It's not your fault."

CHAPTER TWENTY-FOUR

We rode back to the Great City of Eldemy with the remnants of the Lord Field Marshal's army.

Lord Field Marshal Bramstone had fallen in battle, as did many other brave souls.

Jass spoke nary a word during the seven days from the Watchcave to the city. It was for the best, I thought, give her lungs and throat a chance to heal.

As we approached the eastern gates of Eldemy, Xavier rode up next to me and beckoned me to fall behind with him. We were now back among the tattered remains of the foot soldiers. Some wore grim expressions, others expressions of simple shock. A few had reached the point of openly sobbing. The others would join them eventually.

Samana had informed me that their army was outnumbered three-to-one by Marwoleth's. They had been caught in a massive pincer maneuver, being attacked from the front and both flanks.

The two armies became so intermingled, the Lord Field Marshal's artillery was all but ineffective.

She also lamented the absence of Basma, Cardinal Mage of the South and the most powerful war mage in recent history.

It was then that I was struck by the full weight of our actions aboard the Scarab when we engaged the Duchess Adina. Had I not pushed the bow of that ship, perhaps a full volley would have hit us, ending the engagement. Basma would have lived, and perhaps the Lord Field Marshal's army would have bested Marwoleth's impressive array.

Clearly, the Duke, the Lord Field Marshal and the Cardinal Mages had a plan in place before we'd reached Eldemy. Would that plan have succeeded had I not interfered? And how many soldiers would still be alive?

Perhaps, if I had chosen to stay in my comfortable rooms on Ecota Isle, none of this would have happened. Certainly, the crew of the Scarab wouldn't have tried to take the Duchess Adina.

Basma would have made it to Eldemy, and the Lord Field Marshal would have had no need for me to act in his contingency plan.

Torum and Bosul would still be alive, and Jass wouldn't be silent with grief over killing Torum.

Xavier cleared his throat, breaking my line of thought, and I was thankful for it.

"You realize she cannot remain your apprentice," Xavier said kindly but firmly.

I sighed. It hurt, but he was right. I had hoped that adopting an apprentice might raise my stature among the patented mages, but I realized that was a lie.

I was hoping it would raise my own stature with me. It would make me feel like a true and patented mage.

"Yes. I don't have the resources to be a proper mentor. Or the knowledge," I admitted.

"Samana has agreed to take her on as an apprentice. She will put in a word with the Masters of the Collegium," he said.

I nodded, blinking back tears. We sat on our horses as the army slowly marched by. I thought about my life on Ecota Isle. It really was a lovely place, but I missed the busy, chaotic city. I was feared, and sometimes respected, on Ecota Isle, and I got none of that here, but I missed home.

"I'm not cut out to be a mentor," I finally said.

"Perhaps not, but you never know," he said kindly. "The Masters of the Collegium go to great pains to match apprentices to mentors. They want to make sure each apprentice is matched to the right mentor, otherwise, we end up with..." his voice trailed off.

"Situations like this?" I said.

"I suppose so," he admitted.

We rode in silence for a while longer. We were moving slow, and just off the road, so the infantry had passed us, and now horse-drawn cannons passed us one-by-one.

"The Lord Field Marshal's tactics didn't work very well," he said, watching the cannons pass.

"Makes sense," I said, "Marwoleth studied the siege of Eldemy too. It appears he learned lessons from it as well."

Xavier nodded, saying, "and his experience was first-hand."

As the last of the cannon passed, we got back on the road and picked up our pace. The camp followers were nearly a mile behind the troops, so the road was now clear.

"Samana and I agreed to petition the Duke to give you dispensation for breaking your exile," he said.

"That's kind of you, brother," I said smiling faintly.

"It is the least I can do, brother," he said.

"Can I ask you a question?" I asked.

"Of course, but I might not choose to answer it," he said smiling.

"When I used the brass cup, I got Samana. She said you had fallen in battle," I started.

"Did you," I asked directly.

He smiled, but there was sadness there.

"No, I didn't fall," he admitted.

"You were another one of the Lord Field Marshal's contingencies?" I asked.

"I was actually part of yours," he said. "While the Lord Field Marshal trusted you, as I had vouched for you, he didn't trust your abilities, I'm afraid."

There was an apology in Xavier's voice, but the words still stung, even though I knew them to be true.

"And Samana was part of it. She's a good actress," I said glumly.

"Oh no. I was the only one who knew my part in the Lord Field Marshal's plan. Samana was in the dark, and she's none-to-happy about it," Xavier said.

"The Lord Field Marshal didn't trust Samana," I said incredulously.

"Nothing of the sort," Xavier corrected. "Whatever you said to him when we met at the palace scared him. He emerged from that chamber a changed man. In all honesty, the only reason I think he trusted me was that I'm your brother," he said with a chuckle.

We rode back up to the front of the sad procession, and I could see people lining the streets, ready to cheer the victorious army.

To either side of the road, just outside the gates, were two huge bonfires. The wind had picked up, so there wasn't too much smoke, but it was difficult to see the source of the fires.

As I passed them, I saw piles of what I could only assume were ironwood doors. Atop each bonfire were large reinforced ironwood gates. Then I noticed that the eastern gates of the city didn't exist. There was an opening in the wall, but the gigantic gates there were missing, no doubt they were resting on the bonfires.

I smiled to myself. Lord Field Marshal Thuror Bramstone had been a smart and thorough man.

He must have ordered all the doors and gates to be removed and burned. Perhaps he had told the Duke, who would have ordered their dismantling in Bramstone's absence. Perhaps the Duke ordered them set aflame as our victorious army approached, as a sort of tribute.

But I didn't see a lot of celebratory faces among the Lord Field Marshal's army, and I understood why. There were far fewer of them marching back than originally left.

"I don't feel much like celebrating. I think I'll take Jass the long way about and head back to the Bonny Scarecrow. I could use a bath," I said to Xavier.

"I'd join you," he started. "That came out wrong. Not for the bath. We're a bit too old to share a bathtub, I think."

We both laughed.

"I always hated that," I said.

"I hated it more, but mother was trying to save water, and the wood to heat it," he said.

"I just thought it was gross that I was swimming around in your filthy water," I said.

"How do you think I felt?" he said looking at me with that all-too-familiar glare.

We both laughed.

I called for Jass to follow me and we turned south toward the Bonny Scarecrow. Kidal and Dail rode with us.

Xavier called out as we rode away.

"Look me up before you leave, Mandeight. This time we'll have a proper goodbye."

"I shall, brother," I called back. I hoped he was able to smooth over my violation of exile. That would be nice. After all this, I really didn't want to spend the rest of my life in a cell.

The four of us rode in silence for nearly an hour as we wended our way through the narrow streets of the outer city.

Many of the folk in the streets bowed reverently as we passed. They, too, had heard rumor of the battle, but they gave us neither cheers nor adulation, only respect and quiet thanks. They would have had the worst of it if Marwoleth's army had marched on Eldemy, and they knew it. The folk of the outer city were always more respectful of soldiers.

As we approached the Bonny Scarecrow, Kidal stopped suddenly.

"I don't think I want to go to that place right now. I want the other establishment," he said.

I knew just what he was talking about, and it seemed a rather coarse conversation for mixed company.

"Well," I started.

"You want some whoring, don't you, southerner?" Dail interrupted.

"Now just wait a...," I began.

"It's okay, mage. I'll show him the way. I'm a regular," Dail said.

"Dail!" I said, "I'm scandalized!"

She looked at me and smiled.

"Good," she said, and she and Kidal rode off toward carnal bliss.

Jass and I reached the Bonny Scarecrow, gave our mounts over to the stable boy and entered the place in silence.

She didn't want to talk, and I didn't want to force her. Frankly, I didn't want to talk either. I couldn't fathom the pain she was feeling over Torum's death, though I had an inkling of it from Cardinal Mage Basma's death. But Jass's victim, for lack of a better term, was far more personal.

Though we had barely known Bosul and Torum for a fortnight, we had traveled with them. We had eaten with them. We had knowingly ridden into danger with them. We had fought with them.

I knew it would be best for her to talk about it, but I didn't know how to start or what to say. I really was a terrible mentor.

Basil greeted us with his usual feigned formality until he saw Jass's expression.

"Come, my dear. I'll have the maid draw you a bath. Come

along," he said taking her arm gently and leading her slowly up the stairs. He ignored me entirely, and that was fine.

I slumped down at an empty table, and some of the other patrons moved away. I'm sure I smelled vile, but I didn't care.

Basil emerged from upstairs and joined me with a pitcher of brown ale and two cups.

He filled each cup and handed me one, raising it up in toast. I did the same.

He looked me in the eye and said, very seriously, "to surviving."

I nodded to him and we drank. I blinked back tears. Survive. That's about all we had done.

"I'm going to give Jass up to the Collegium," I said. "I don't have the skill nor disposition to be a mentor to her."

Basil nodded but said nothing, like a good bartender.

"She'll do much better there. She'll learn the discipline that I can't teach her, and she'll need it. She's going to become very powerful," I said trying to justify my decision to myself.

"She's does seem to have a good head on her shoulders," he mused.

"I don't have the money to pay off my account," I said.

He gave me a wry smile. "I didn't think you would," Basil said.

"I can put her up here between terms at the Collegium, at least until she starts earning, though I may put her to work in the evenings. I don't want her thinking everything in life is free," Basil mused.

"That's good of you, Basil," I said.

"So what happened? We heard rumors of an army assembling to the East when the Lord Field Marshal left with his retinue, but nothing else," he said.

I told him the whole story. The meeting with the Lord Field Marshal, the ride north to Ecoja Smurt, the swift ride to the Watchcave and all the events that happened there.

"That poor girl," he whispered when I finished. "No sign of her mother, then?"

"No," I said.

"And this Marwoleth is dead?" Basil asked.

I laughed bitterly. "I doubt it."

We finished the pitcher, and Basil called for another.

"It's strange," I started.

"What's strange?" Basil asked.

"This Marwoleth. He wasn't at all what I was expecting," I explained.

"How so?" he asked.

"Well, he wasn't a raving lunatic," I began. "Someone so steeped in dark magic, someone capable of killing thousands of people and perverting their remains into that sick farce of an army. You would think someone capable of that would be utterly insane."

"I would think so," Basil said.

"But he wasn't. Not at all," I said.

"How did he behave?" Basil asked.

"That's the thing. He was ... polite, friendly even. He didn't torture us. He didn't threaten us. He fed us. He even joked with us," I said.

"That is strange," Basil said.

"And I think it was more frightening than if he had been a madman," I said. "That someone capable of such ... darkness could seem so utterly normal. Had circumstances been different, I could see him being a friend."

"Makes you wonder if we're all capable of such things?" Basil asked.

"Yes. That's what concerns me," I said, and I quietly wondered about the missing Forces of magic. Were there more?

And if we had access to that forbidden knowledge, would we all end up like Marwoleth?

CHAPTER TWENTY-FIVE

The next morning, I escorted Jass to the Citadel of the Cardinal Mage of the West, the home of my brother.

I informed her along the way that Samana had arranged a place for her in the Collegium, and that she would be her new mentor.

Jass only nodded her face remaining expressionless.

As we rode through the city, we could see the remnants of celebration.

Each of the Cardinal Mages' citadels displayed beautiful Eldemic architecture. In fact, they were miniature replicas of the duke's palace, with turrets, white stone from High Fall, defensive walls.

We were led into the citadel and up one of the turrets to Xavier's workroom. It was large and palatial, with large windows letting in the breeze of early Spring.

Shelves lined the walls, filled with large, leather-bound tomes. What I wouldn't give for a week in that room unsupervised.

Two large tables dominated the center of the room. Upon them were pages and pages of writing, piles of books and a few trinkets strewn about.

Samana and Xavier were both there.

"Welcome, Mandeight, and to you as well, Apprentice Jass," Xavier said as we emerged from the stairwell.

"Xavier. Samana," I said nodding to each.

Jass said nothing. She crossed the room and stood next to

Samana, looking down at the floor.

"She knows?" Samana asked.

"Yes, I told her," I said with no small amount of shame.

Samana stood and put an arm around Jass and said, "are you ready to go, Jass?" She nodded and they headed for the stairwell.

As she passed me, she put a hand on my arm and said, "she'll be alright."

They left.

Xavier cleared his throat, and I wiped my eyes.

"I have a few things to discuss with you, brother," Xavier said motioning to a chair at one of the large tables. Then he sat down.

"First thing's first," and he tossed a coin-filled pouch across the table. It landed before me with a muffled ring of coin.

"That's your compensation," he said. "I spoke with the exchequer, and he agreed to double what he intended to pay. You'll find it's quite a sum."

I picked the pouch up and hefted it with one hand. It was heavy. There was gold in that pouch. I put it in my purse.

"What else?" I asked.

He smiled, producing a leather folio from beneath scattered parchment on his table. I recognize it instantly. It was the same sort of folio that held Patents of Magic. Tooled into the leather was the symbol of the Collegium, a series of intersecting triangles.

"You can't be serious," I said with disbelief.

"It took some convincing, and Samana was far more insistent than I, I should mention. But yes, these are your Patents of Magic," he said sliding the folio across the table.

I unwound the leather cord from around the button on the front and opened it. I read the cover page:

"Be it known that Mandeight Birdstaff is a fully patented mage of the Sovereign Duchy of Eldemy, as confirmed by the Masters of the Collegium and approved by His Grace Duke Elkis the 434th."

"I don't believe it," I said looking up from the folio.

"They are true and legal patents," Xavier insisted. "I even asked His Grace to sign them personally, which he did. That is his signature, by his own hand."

"So my exile is ended?" I asked.

"Not quite. Your exile has been stayed, on a probationary basis. You must present yourself to the Collegium or one of the Cardinal Mages whenever you come to Eldemy. And at some point, in the future, at a time of your choosing, you'll stand before the Masters of the Collegium for your graduating inquiry, your trials. If you pass that, your exile will be permanently lifted," he said.

Then he stood and extended his hand, saying, "Congratulations, brother."

I stood and we shook hands. "Thank you, brother."

He sat back down and began rummaging through the clutter on the table.

"There is one more thing I want to discuss with you. Ah, here it is," he said producing a small stone pendant hanging from a silver chain.

"What do you make of this?" he said tossing it to me.

I looked down and carved into the stone was the symbol for the Force of undeath, or spirit or soul, as Marwoleth called it.

I summoned the Force of magic and examined it.

"This is intricate work. I've never seen anything like it, except for that object in the cavern. Did you have a look at that?" I asked.

"I did. It was mounted to the cavern floor, and we couldn't remove it, much like the large spyglass. There were very intricate enchantments holding both artifacts in place, and if we tried to break them, we would have broken the other enchantments, rendering the objects useless," Xavier explained.

I examined the spells of the pendant again.

"There are magical links within this enchantment," I said. "Gods... more than I can count."

"Yes, you are correct, unfortunately," Xavier said.

"You found this on Marwoleth," I said in sudden realization.

"Just so," Xavier confirmed. "His spirit, or soul, seems to be connected to others through this somehow."

"I figured that wasn't the end of him, down there smashed on the rocks," I said with a frown.

"Correct. No chance of that at all," Xavier said grimly.

"So there are more ... of him?" I asked.

"It appears there might be many more of him," Xavier said. "And it's very likely the rest know that this one fell. Though I suppose it's possible that he was the last."

"But why would he bother wearing this then?" I asked.

"Exactly. Wishful thinking at its worst. He'll be back, no doubt of that," Xavier said.

"He called the Force of undeath the Force of spirit or soul," I said.

"He could be correct," Xavier said. "We know little of that Force."

"He had mastery of other Forces," I said. "He could render himself and his undead invisible. I suspect using something like a Force of light."

"Really?" Xavier said genuinely surprised. Then realization washed over his face, much as it had mine. "It seems rather obvious now that there would be such a Force."

"Yes, it does, doesn't it?" I said. "But we know nothing of it, and it isn't taught at the Collegium."

"That does seem strange," Xavier mused.

The two of us mused over this for a while, then I remembered what Marwoleth had said about the Patents of Magic and Forces we weren't allowed to learn.

"What do we know of the proceedings when the Patents of Magic were established?" I asked.

"Very little, I'm afraid," Xavier admitted. "We know such a law was passed, and that the verbiage of the patents were written, and that the Masters of the Collegium were granted the right to present them. Other than that, very little is known. I've seen no record of the deliberations or debates. No record of discussions between the Masters and the Duke's viziers."

"Doesn't that seem strange to you?" I asked.

"It does. You think the Force of light was intentionally removed from the curriculum," he said.

"That's one explanation, and probably the most likely," I said.

"That's something worth investigating, I think," he said.

"As do I," I agreed.

I wondered if the Masters of the Collegium, back when the Patents of Magic were established, had to agree to remove certain subjects from their curriculum. It seemed likely. Was that knowledge lost? Or did the Masters of the Collegium secretly preserve it? It seemed unlikely they would let such knowledge die through the generations, even if it was forbidden.

Then my mind drifted back to the Watchcave, thinking of my brief conversations with Marwoleth. Xavier eyed me suspiciously.

"What is it," he finally asked.

"I spoke with Marwoleth," I started, "he called himself an archmage, and he wasn't joking."

Xavier frowned, and he nodded slightly.

"The term 'archmage' was once used to describe certain mages, but you have to go back to rather old texts, and they're very rare," Xavier admitted.

"So there once were archmages?" I asked.

"Yes. I found one reference from the siege of Eldemy that referred to 'Archmage Marwoleth,'" Xavier said. "And there are a few earlier references to the term."

"So the Patents of Magic were established to prevent archmages," I said not really asking a question.

"It appears so," Xavier answered.

CHAPTER TWENTY-SIX

After Xavier and I said our goodbyes, and he made me promise to write our mother, I headed back to the Bonny Scarecrow to prepare for my voyage home.

Kidal and Dail sat in the dining room, obviously well-sated from their trip to the dodgier part of town. They were drinking ale and picking at their lunch when I sat down.

"What's next, Mandeight?" Kidal said.

"I'm going to head home, I think," I said.

"Are you sure you have to?" Dail asked, looking at my new Patents of Magic, which I had sat on the table.

"I do, at least for a while. Most of my possessions are there, including my library," I explained.

"Mind if I come along?" Kidal asked.

"Not at all. I wouldn't mind the company," I said smiling. My life on Ecota Isle had been lonely since I was the only mage there. Most of the people I interacted with there were business associates, not friends. Not to mention the fact that everyone else was either a pirate, former pirate or someone who catered to pirates.

"What about you, assassin?" Kidal teased, "you want to come too?"

"Where is your home?" she asked.

"Ecota Isle. It's one of the Outer Isles," I explained. "It's quite nice. Never snows. Only the occasional rainstorm."

"Maybe. I think I've had my last contract for a while," she mused. She seemed melancholy, but I knew better than to ask why.

After much cajoling from Kidal, Dail agreed to join us. We agreed to book passage as soon as possible.

Once I was in my room, I remembered the coin purse Xavier had given me. I opened it to discover that there was gold in there. In fact, there was nothing but gold. It was a literal fortune.

The next morning, I announced to Kidal and Dail that I would go find us passage and that they should enjoy themselves at the Bonny Scarecrow.

I settled my account with Basil and gave him a little extra to take care of Kidal and Dail while I was gone. I then headed to the docks, but not the outer dock, I went to Eldemy.

It took me most of the day to find what I was looking for, and by the time I returned, it was time for dinner.

Basil had laid out for us a veritable feast, filled with puddings and roasted vegetables, and dominating the table was a whole roasted piglet.

"I booked us a ship," I announced as the others ate.

"What's her name?" Kidal asked.

"I don't know, but she's due here tomorrow. She's in the Eldemy docks now, but they'll stop here," I said.

Kidal and Dail looked at each other. "You don't know the name of the ship? Are you sure there is a ship? I think you got robbed," Kidal said.

"Same here," Dail added.

"I didn't get robbed," I insisted. "I just didn't get the name."

Kidal dropped his fork and said, "You, Mandeight, are an amateur."

"If you say so," I said with a smile.

The next morning demonstrated how much of a fortune Xavier had given me.

As we arrived at the docks, the temporary crew was mooring my ship to the dock. Yes, my ship. She was a twin-masted vessel. I believe the man I purchased her from called her a caravel. She had eight twelve-pound guns on the deck and a good-sized hold. Room for plenty of cargo.

"There she is," I said pointing to my newest purchase as we approached.

Kidal walked back and forth along the dock, surveying her with an experienced eye.

"There's no name on the stern," he said. "Even pirates name their ships. Who the hell runs this boat?" he demanded.

"I do. Well actually, you do, if you will be her captain for me," I said.

"What?" Kidal said.

"He bought a boat, but he's too clever to just say it, southerner," Dail said immediately piecing all the facts together.

"Exactly right," I declared, extending my arms to present the ship.

Kidal guffawed and clambered aboard. He started at the stern and slowly made his way forward, inspecting every inch of the new vessel.

"She's in good shape and well-maintained. She'll serve us well," Kidal finally declared.

"She better be. She's new," I called to him.

Dail and I stood at the bottom of the gangway.

"Permission to come aboard, captain," I shouted.

"Permission granted," he laughed.

Once we were all aboard, I presented Kidal with papers.

"This states that you are twenty-five percent owner of this vessel," I said handing him the papers.

I produced a second set and handed them to Dail. "And here are yours. Twenty-five percent as well."

"Thank you, mage. That's very generous of you," she said. She was honestly surprised.

Kidal simply gave me a gigantic hug.

"She needs a name," Dail said.

"I've been racking my brain, but I can't think of an appropriate name," I said with a sigh.

"The Terror!" Kidal said.

"No! This won't be a pirate vessel! Legitimate cargo only!" I said sternly. I was done consorting with pirates.

"That sounds boring," Kidal said.

"We could do with some boring," Dail said. Kidal nodded in agreement.

"The Silence?" Dail suggested.

I frowned at her.

"Unless we're all going to die and turn her into a ghost ship, I don't think so," I said.

"Well, pick a name. You own half of her," Dail said.

"No, I don't. I own twenty-five percent," I said.

"Who owns the other twenty-five percent? The financier?" Kidal asked.

"No. We own her outright. Paid in full," I declared.

"Then who owns the other quarter?" Dail demanded.

"Jass. I'll send a messenger with her share of the profits," I said.

"That'll give her a leg up on life," Dail said. "If we can keep her profitable, that is."

"I got it!" Kidal exclaimed.

"What's that?" I asked.

"The name. Let's call her the Apprentice," he said.

I smiled broadly as tears welled up in my eyes, but I didn't bother hiding them.

"That's a grand name," I said happily. "A grand name indeed."

EPILOGUE

Kidal spent the rest of the day interviewing and hiring crewmen, and the next morning we set sail for home, but I informed Captain Kidal that we needed to make a detour to Lovers' Isle.

Kidal, Dail and I made it to my magically concealed cottage there and we entered. The ornate mirror was just where I left it.

"Let's get it out of here," Kidal said, preparing for some heavy lifting.

"Not just yet. I need to check something," I said. "That covered object in the cavern in the Watchcave was a mirror as well. The enchantment seemed familiar, but I couldn't remember where I'd seen it before."

"It was probably this mirror," Kidal said.

"No. I don't think so. I think it was one of those orbs," I said walking over to the small wooden chest.

I looked at each of the orbs while calling the Force of magic. The intricate tendrils of their ancient enchantments became visible, and one stood out as familiar.

"It's this one," I said carefully picking up one of the glass orbs. Within the glass, I could see swirling gold smoke.

"I wonder..." I mused, placing the orb in the small holder to the right of the mirror.

Suddenly, our images disappeared from the mirror, as did the interior of my cottage. It had transformed from a mirror to a dull silver surface, but it now showed no reflection.

"What did it do?" Kidal asked.

"I have no idea," I said, reaching out to touch the surface of the mirror, and much to my surprise, my hand went through it and disappeared.

"Interesting," I said.

Dail and Kidal looked at me cautiously. I pulled my hand out, and it was unharmed. I gave a shrug and stuck my head through.

"I don't believe it," I said, once I'd pulled my head out of the mirror.

"What?" they both asked.

"Follow me," I said, then I walked through the mirror. Dail and Kidal cautiously followed.

"Are you kidding me?" Dail exclaimed.

Kidal was laughing so hard he had to sit on the stone floor of the cavern, the very same cavern where we were held prisoner by Marwoleth.

We had emerged from my mirror on Lovers' Isle to the mirror in the corner of the cavern in the Watchcave.

"This would have come in handy," Dail said glaring at me with fury.

Yes, it would have, I thought. Now I understood why Cardinal Mage Basma was transporting his mirror to Eldemy. He knew, or at least suspected, that one of the orbs was tied to the mirror in the Watchcave.

That whole ordeal could have been avoided. Basma could have sent assassins, mages, soldiers, anyone he liked, through this mirror to take out Marwoleth. He could have tossed a lit powder keg through and just blown up Marwoleth's undead guards.

Kidal's laughter ceased as he came to the same conclusion.

"I had no way of knowing this," I said hastily. "We were in a hurry when we dropped it off here. If I had known, believe me, we would have used it. I promise you."

Dail still scowled at me. Perhaps she had been informed of Basma's plan. Word of Basma's death had finally reached Eldemy just prior to our departure.

"One day, you'll have to tell me how you came into possession of that mirror," Dail said accusingly.

"What makes you think I'll ever have to tell you anything, assassin," I said. This exchange was familiar, but the roles were reversed. I had once pried into her mysterious path, and now she was prying into mine.

She eyed me suspiciously.

"Very well," she finally said.

I looked around the cavern. The bodies of the undead guards had been removed, along with Torum's remains, though the thousands of bones on the floor remained.

"You think the other orbs lead to other places?" Kidal asked.

"Probably," I said. "The enchantments on that golden orb stood out as somewhat similar to the ones on this mirror. The others are probably tied to other mirrors," I suggested.

"Where do you think they lead?" Dail asked.

"That's a good question, and one we'll answer when we and that mirror are safe on Ecota Isle," I said.

"This will be exciting," Kidal said.

"Not too exciting, I hope."

AFTERWORD

The character of Mandeight Birdstaff was an NPC in my long-running Dungeons and Dragons campaign.

The Duchy of Eldemy was the setting for that campaign.

By the time of the campaign, Mandeight was a semi-retired mage with knowledge of many dark magical powers. While he was never the villain in that game, he was certainly a dangerous, if affable, fellow.

The Mandeight Chronicles are in essence his origin story. It all started as a thought exercise that turned into a series of novels.

If you've enjoyed reading this novel, I would ask that you tell your friends.

ABOUT THE AUTHOR

Stu Venable

Stu Venable was born in Long Beach, California and holds a degree in Journalism from California State University, Long Beach. He's been a fan of fantasy and science fiction since reading The Hobbit during the summer between grammar school and middle school. He is the father to two children and has two dogs. This is his first published novel.

BOOKS IN THIS SERIES

The Mandeight Chronicles

Mandeight is a capable mage, but his insatiable curiosity concerns his peers. Early in his magical education, Mandeight was marked as a potential "dark mage," and while he does redeem himself, some wonder if that potential dark mage is in there somewhere.

Mandeight And The Apprentice Mage

Mandeight could have lived a life of leisure and influence as a mage of the Duchy of Eldemy, but that wasn't in the cards. Exiled on a remote island for nearly twenty years, he discovers the workings of a dangerous and ancient necromancer. In order to stop him, he must return to the one place where he is not welcome.

Mandeight The Patented Mage

When Mandeight set sail for Eldemy, he was intending to display his magical abilities for his trials at the Collegium Magicum, but others had a different sort of trial in mind.
Mandeight's past misdeeds have come back to haunt him, and his former apprentice might have to pay the price.

Printed in Great Britain
by Amazon